HONOR'S FALL

Lost in thought as she walked, Honor did not see Edmond coming. Startled as they collided, she lost her footing and tumbled to the garden path.

Garden path, indeed, she thought, as she felt herself being lifted to her feet and held in arms that felt almost as hard as her landing place.

"Are you hurt?" Edmond asked.

"Let me go," she responded, pushing him away and stepping back a pace. "Must you maul me about?"

"Maul you about?" said Edmond, then paused in his declaration of innocence to view the anger warming her cheeks, the fire sparkling in her magnificent eyes. He recalled the other day, when she had tumbled into his bed and he had nipped her earlobe softly and followed that with little kisses, working his way toward her mouth. He had not really thought of that as mauling, nor did he now, as he caught her by the shoulders, then slowly pulled her against his chest, enfolding her.

"Why do you find this so unpleasant?" he said, as he held her chin between thumb and forefinger so she could not turn away. "Tell me—and I promise I will never bother you again."

The
Honorable
Thief

Martha Kirkland

A SIGNET BOOK

SIGNET
Published by the Penguin Group
Penguin Books USA Inc., 375 Hudson Street,
New York, New York 10014, U.S.A.
Penguin Books Ltd, 27 Wrights Lane,
London W8 5TZ, England
Penguin Books Australia Ltd, Ringwood,
Victoria, Australia
Penguin Books Canada Ltd, 10 Alcorn Avenue,
Toronto, Ontario, Canada M4V 3B2
Penguin Books (N.Z.) Ltd, 182–190 Wairau Road,
Auckland 10, New Zealand

Penguin Books Ltd, Registered Offices:
Harmondsworth, Middlesex, England

First published by Signet, an imprint of Dutton Signet,
a division of Penguin Books USA Inc.

First Printing, December, 1996
10 9 8 7 6 5 4 3 2 1

 REGISTERED TRADEMARK—MARCA REGISTRADA

Printed in the United States of America

With love for my dear neighbor,
Mrs. Jane Smith, and for her Edmond

Chapter 1

The speeding post chaise swerved to the left, and as its outer wheels deserted the icy ground, the lone passenger, his rough-hewn face flush with fever, was sent crashing against the none-too-clean squabs. For endless seconds the coach wobbled, flirting with disaster, before all four wheels finally found the road once again. The sudden lurch tossed the man forward, and as his head hit the side of the door, myriad shards of pain pierced his brain.

Edmond James Lawrence grabbed his aching head as if to keep it from falling off his shoulders. When he moaned, the sound seemed to come from a far distance, as though someone other than himself had protested the unending assault upon his pain-racked body.

Not for the first time in this never-ending journey, he questioned what evil genius had prompted him to leave London on a bitter cold Sunday afternoon. And for what? To undertake a trip he had postponed at least a dozen times these past seven months. One hundred and seventy-six miles so far, and it wanted at least another two hours before he reached Abbingdon.

If he lived long enough to reach Abbingdon!

He was ill. Easy to see that now, of course. Now that

he was agonizingly sober. He had endured more than seventeen hours in one bone-rattling "Yellow Bounder" after another, with their poorly fitted windows and their excess of sour-smelling straw upon the floor, and the numbing effect of the large quantity of brandy he had consumed while at the card table had long since worn off.

It had all started Saturday night with a rubber of whist at White's. Friendly enough at the outset, at some point the game had changed tempo; the play became deep, the players intense. As the game reached a fever pitch, Edmond began to experience the unmistakable signs of fever of another sort. With the impatience of the chronically healthy, he disregarded the warnings, and by the time the sun peeped through the heavy brocade curtains at the windows of the card room, the inside of his throat felt like emery paper, while his eyes seemed dry as desert sand.

At the insistence of his life-long friend, Sidney Avery, the game was suspended long enough for the players to adjourn from St. James's Street to Avery's bachelor establishment at number twelve Chesterfield Street. Edmond wanted nothing more than to go to his own lodgings and seek the comfort of his bed, but being the major winner, he could not in good conscience beg off from continuing play.

Never one to partake heavily of strong spirits, he had been so unwise as to avail himself of the decanter Avery's valet set in the middle of the baize-covered table. For medicinal purposes, he told himself. Because the brandy seemed to take the edge off the roughness of his throat and the pounding inside his head, he sipped one glass after another, and by the time his fellow players finally declared the game at an end, Edmond was drunk as a lord.

It was the wisdom of drink that prompted him to gather his winnings and announce his intention of traveling to Devon that very moment to visit his recently inherited estate. Unfortunately, the idiotic notion was heartily seconded by his equally inebriated cronies. Further jug-shrewdness prompted him to bypass his own bachelor quarters and his well-sprung carriage and seek instead the dubious comforts of the hired chaise.

The first few stages of the journey were, blessedly, a blur, and since the traveler had no luggage, removing to a new coach when the horses were exchanged required only that he be helped out of one vehicle and into another. He had not entered even one of the posting inns, nor had he partaken of food or drink since the wretched ordeal began.

Not that Edmond wanted food. Firmly believing he would never swallow again without pain, all he desired was a warm bed, preferably one that did not rock and lurch and throw him about until he thought his skull would burst open like a ripe melon.

At the Golden Hind, at Exeter, when he tried to make his burning throat work long enough to tell the ostler to help him inside, that he needed to rest, Edmond had been unable to make himself understood. Neither the ostler nor the postilion had paid any heed to his attempts at speech. Assuming the passenger was still inebriated, and interested only in claiming his tip and getting in out of the cold, the young man had merely hustled Edmond into another "Yellow Bounder," collected his money, and sped the new postboy on his way. And from the wild ride Edmond was experiencing on this last leg of the journey, he suspected the latest lad was not an experienced postboy at all, but a caddie in training.

That disquieting thought had only just occurred to the

traveler when the speeding coach rounded a particularly sharp bend, swerving once again. This time, however, when the wheels lifted off the ground, tossing Edmond against the squabs, there was no interim wobble followed by a lurching recovery. This time the coach seemed to glide like an ice skater, albeit a listing one, until it finally toppled over onto its side.

The last thing Edmond remembered was the excruciating blow dealt his shoulder when he was thrown against the roof.

The ancient leather valise Miss Honoria Danforth carried contained only her nightclothes and a few personal items, but it was getting heavier by the minute. And judging by the little enameled watch pinned at the front of the woolen guimpe she had donned for extra warmth, she had been walking for two hours' worth of minutes. Setting the valise down upon the snow-covered ground, she wiggled the cramped fingers of her left hand, shaking the right as well, knowing that soon it, too, would be crying out for relief.

Her fingers were stiff with cold. It had begun to snow again about an hour ago, and the tan kid gloves Uncle Wesley had sent her for Christmas were soaked through, as were her half boots, the hem of her maroon kerseymere skirt, and the cape of her brown wool redingote.

Some poet had once likened walking upon new-fallen snow to treading upon white velvet. Honor was beginning to suspect the fanciful fellow was a Bedlamite; either that or he had never trudged for miles along a rutted country lane where holes lay in wait to trap the unwary. More than once Honor had stepped upon what appeared to be solid ground only to sink to her boot tops, a circumstance that allowed the icy powder to spill over into her shoes where it melted and soaked her stockings.

Aside from her concern for the obvious dangers of wet feet, and her wish to be inside, shielded from the biting January cold, Honor was beginning to fear that she was lost. Bascomb Manor was situated a scant three miles from Lower Chidderton; surely she should have come to the little village by now. At least she should have if she had made the correct decision a mile back when the road forked.

She had been to Lower Chidderton only once before, and that was four weeks ago, when she traveled from London to begin her employment as governess to the Bascomb's daughter, Ivy. When the stagecoach set her down at the village, the Bascomb's landau had been waiting to convey her directly to the manor house. Because she had been heartily sick of travel by that time, she had paid little attention to the route taken. During her brief employment, almost constant inclement weather had kept her and her young charge from venturing any farther than the end of the snow-packed carriageway.

Foolish beyond permission! Honor saw that now. But how was she to have foreseen that one day she would be required to find her way to the village alone? In her wildest dreams she had never expected to be turned out. A pariah. With everyone in the house forbidden to so much as speak to her.

Embarrassment warmed her cheeks as she recalled the angry words, the vitriol that had poured from Mrs. Bascomb's mouth during that final, humiliating confrontation in the over-furnished drawing room. Mortified at being sacked, Honor had been obliged to swallow her pride and seek out her employer, to ask for her wages.

"Wages!"

Not caring who heard her, the woman had shrieked like the parvenu she was, her angry brown eyes resembling those of some wild creature, her face mottled purple with rage. "Not so much as a farthing!" she yelled. "Not until I have had time to look about the house. A Jezebel who would practice her wiles upon an innocent, God-fearing young man would think nothing of helping herself to any article of value that struck her fancy."

Honor seethed inwardly at this latest allegation, only just controlling her desire to turn and sweep from the room. But as much as she might wish to walk away, she could not afford the luxury of pride. She needed her wages. And she needed them now.

Reasoning with the sanctimonious harridan was a waste of breath; Honor had come to that conclusion the night before when Mrs. Bascomb discovered her at the bottom of the servants' stairs, trying to fend off the unwanted advances of her employer's nineteen-year-old nephew.

Honor had just dealt the insolent young pup a resounding blow to his left ear when his aunt walked in upon the scene. All the evidence to the contrary, Mrs. Bascomb had chosen to believe that the governess had enticed the young man to seek her out.

In the cold light of day, aware that reason played little part in her employer's makeup, Honor had called upon every ounce of dignity she possessed. "I must have what is owed me," she said evenly. "As well, the contract I signed before coming to Devon promised a return ticket to London when my services were no longer needed. The agency—"

"Do not mention the agency to me!" Mrs. Bascomb said. "They shall hear from me soon enough, for I specifically asked for a governess of good character. And one of mature years, I might add." Her corseted bosom heaved with indignation. "Do not think you pulled the wool over my eyes by insisting that you were nine and twenty, for I did not believe you. Not for an instant. Four and twenty is more like it, or I miss my guess. In sending you, the agency has already broken the contract, so I see no reason why *I* must abide by its terms."

"It is the ethical thing to do," Honor had replied quietly. "I should think that would be reason enough, for—"

"Silence! I will not be spoken to in that insolent manner. If anything is owed you, I will send it to the agency at their London address. Now leave my house." The conversation at an end, Mrs. Bascomb had walked to the door and yelled for the butler. "Jessup!"

"Yes, madam?" The servant answered so quickly Honor felt certain he had been loitering in the vestibule listening with pleasure as the governess received her dismissal.

"Miss Danforth is leaving now. Show her to the door."

"Shall I summon John Coachman, madam?"

"No," she replied. "That will not be necessary."

Honor gasped, unable to believe her ears. "But surely I am to be driven to the village. What of my trunk?"

The older woman ignored her as if she had not spoken. "See that Miss Danforth leaves the premises immediately, Jessup. If it should become necessary, remove her by force."

Unwilling to discover if the butler would obey his employer to the letter, Honor had gathered the tatters of her pride, donned her redingote, then picked up her valise and left the house, her head held high.

Now, however, she was wet and cold, and more frightened than she wanted to admit. There was ample reason to be afraid, for her reticule contained exactly one golden guinea and a six-pence, and a ticket on the stagecoach to London would cost her just under five pounds.

Not that she could actually go home, of course, not when she knew the threat her being there posed to her beloved Uncle Wesley. No, she had left his home to protect him, and she would not risk returning to him.

That left her with only one option. As much as she disliked the idea, she would be obliged to go to Mrs. Milson, the nurse who had cared for her mother during her final illness, and see if that dear soul was willing to hide her for a time.

"London?" Honor said aloud. "Honoria Danforth, you do not even know how to get to the village."

The sound of her voice frightened a bushy-tailed red squirrel whose hurried retreat from a nearby tree limb sent a clump of snow down upon the speaker's wide-poked bonnet. Oddly enough, the unexpected snowball had a cheering effect upon Honor, and for the first time that day she smiled.

Watching the animal scurry to a higher branch, she called out, "Is that what passes for help from above in this neighborhood? A snowball to my best bonnet?"

Her only answer was a series of agitated chirps and whistles from the squirrel, the noises seeming overloud in the hushed whiteness of the landscape. Still, the encounter made Honor feel less alone, and for that she was grateful. "If that is an omen," she murmured, "warning me to stop feeling sorry for myself and get moving, I think I would do well to heed the message."

The words said, she leaned forward and brushed the snow off the poke of the chocolate brown velvet, pushed a stray lock of even darker brown hair beneath the crown of the hat, then lifted her valise and trudged onward, vowing to turn back and retrace her steps if she saw nothing within the next fifteen minutes. Her self-imposed time limit had almost expired when she rounded a sharp bend in the road and saw an overturned post chaise, its bright yellow sides almost invisible beneath a blanket of freshly fallen snow.

Hurrying to the vehicle, she checked first to see if the postboy was injured. There was no sign of him, but judging by the hoofprints in the snow and the fact that both horses were gone, she assumed the fellow had unhitched the team and ridden to the village for help. Since there was no evidence of passengers, she decided the coach must be empty, and was about to follow in the direction of the hoofprints when she heard a muffled moan.

Using her valise as a stepping stool, Honor climbed up onto the carriage so she could look through the window. To her surprise, she discovered a man inside the coach, and though he wore an expensively tailored wool greatcoat that should have kept him warn, he shivered as though suffering from an ague.

From the little she could see of him through the dirty glass, he appeared youngish—probably no more than thirty—with thick, dark brown hair and at least a day's worth of whiskers shadowing his face. His eyelids were closed, and as he turned his head from side to side, he moaned as if in great pain.

"Sir," she called through the window, "can you hear me? Are you injured?"

When he made no reply, Honor struggled to wrest the door open, then more or less fell into the coach beside the passenger, her skirts tossed about her legs in a most indecorous display. As she straightened her clothing, she noticed that the gentleman had grown still, and fearing that he might be dead, she yanked open his greatcoat and thrust her hand inside his waistcoat to check his heart for a beat.

"Thank God," she said when she felt a strong pulse against her gloved palm.

After ascertaining the all-important information that he still lived, Honor took a moment to assimilate two rather surprising facts. The first, that beneath his greatcoat the gentleman wore evening clothes. The second, and by far the most interesting, that her searching hand had disturbed a pocketbook fairly bulging with money.

She gasped. The pocketbook, fashioned of smooth, rich leather, had slipped from inside the man's coat and lay only inches from her fingertips. For what seemed like an eternity she stared at the object, unable to move, while a battle waged inside her head—her basic honesty fighting with her desire for survival.

In the end her need to survive prevailed. But not without inflicting painful wounds upon her self-respect. Feeling little better than a thief, she reached for the pocketbook and made a cursory count of its contents. Her breath caught in her throat, for the total was in excess of a thousand pounds.

Promising herself that she would repay the loan with interest, she removed a five-pound note, then set the pocketbook in her lap while she searched inside the man's waistcoat for his card case. She knew that gentlemen always carried calling cards, and she would need his name and address in order to return the five pounds.

Finding the small, gold case, she withdrew one crisp white card, read the name on it, then placed the card and the five-pound note in her reticule. She returned the gold case to the man's waistcoat, then with the pocketbook in hand, she was searching out its original place in his coat when the rescuers arrived.

The snow must have muffled the sound of the horses' hooves, for only when the coach shook did she look up to discover the man staring at her through the open door. His white beaver hat and yellow jacket identified him as a postboy, but even so, Honor jumped when she saw him.

To her horror, her jerky motion caused the leather pocketbook to fly out of her damp fingers. It flew across the coach as if it had wings, and as it traveled, the cache of pound notes fell out, drifting through the air like so many snowflakes.

Honor's face must have registered the guilt she felt, for the postboy's eyes, as big as saucers when he had spied the money, slowly narrowed with suspicion.

" 'Ere," he said, "wot's this?"

"What's amiss, young Davey?" another, older man called out.

The postboy turned to look over his shoulder at the speaker. "When the caddie come riding in to the yard at the Ram, 'e did say as 'ow there bain't but one passenger, didn't 'e?"

"Right you are. Just the one gentleman. Bound for Abbingdon."

"Well, summit's not right, for there be two people in 'ere now."

"It's daft you are, young Davey. Passengers don't multiply in route."

The older man laughed as though he had made a joke, but the postboy did not even smile. "Daft I may be, but I know 'ow to count. And there be two people in this 'ere coach now. And only one of 'em be a gentleman."

His accusing glance raked Honor from her bedraggled

bonnet down to her wet hem and boots. "And wot's more," he said, "I caught 'er going through the gentleman's pockets. Already nabbed 'is pocketbook, she 'ad, and you'll not believe the money wot's flung about in 'ere."

"Did you say, 'She?' "

"You 'eard me," he answered. "Caught 'er red-'anded, I did."

Honor knew a moment of panic. *Red-handed* was exactly what she was, and if she could not convince these two fellows that she was not robbing the gentleman, she would find herself tossed into the Lower Chidderton lockup before the day was over. Or even—heaven forbid—confined in the stocks like any common criminal. "You . . . you are mistaken," she sputtered. "I was just—"

"You was just robbin' an injured man," the postboy said. "I know what I saw."

"Bring her out here to the wagon, young Davey. We'll tie her up good and tight, then after we take the injured gentleman to the Ram, we'll haul her over to Squire Clegg's and let him decide what's to be done with her."

"A good idea," the postboy said.

He reached his hand toward Honor as though to catch hold of her and drag her from the chaise, but she pushed back against the squabs as far as possible, avoiding his grasp.

"Do not touch me!" she said. "I tell you, you are making a mistake. I am not a thief, I . . . I . . ." Honor uttered the first words that popped into her head. "I am the gentleman's wife." Recalling the name on the card, she said, "I am Mrs. Edmond Lawrence."

Chapter 2

"Give him all the barley water he will drink," the doctor said, indicating the blue willow jug on the bedside table, "and see he stays warm."

The kindly old man, so frail and bent Honor wondered how he continued to care for his patients, poured some of the water into a glass and added a drop of brownish liquid from a small green apothecary bottle. "Tincture of opium," he said, setting the bottle beside the jug of barley water. "It should help if he becomes too restive. But use it sparingly. No more than a drop every few hours."

Closing his bag, he retrieved his hat and surtout from the tapestried slipper chair where he had dropped them earlier, then inched his way to the bedroom door where the innkeeper waited to help him down the stairs. As he passed Honor, he patted her shoulder in an avuncular manner.

"The next few days may be difficult, my dear, but your husband is a strong, healthy man. Have no fear, it will take more than a bout of influenza to put that one in his grave."

Honor forced a smile to her lips, though her cheeks felt uncomfortably warm at the misplaced sympathy given her by the saintly old man. Believing that she was the patient's wife, the doctor had naturally assumed she would be worried, and had tried to ease her anxiety. For her part, it had been all Honor could do to look the kindly gentleman in the face, knowing she was voicing more lies with every breath she took.

The moment the door clicked shut, she leaned her back against the wooden panels and closed her eyes. Her entire body trembled with reaction. *A few days,* the doctor had said. Mr. Edmond Lawrence might well be out of his head for a few days. She breathed easier at the thought.

Not that she wished the gentleman any ill fortune! Far from it. But she had not, after all, had anything to do with his contracting influenza. All she had done was stop to help an unfortunate traveler. Of course, if she had not helped *herself* to five pounds from the traveler's pocketbook, she would not be in her current predicament, nor would she be in need of a few days' grace.

It would take time to allay the suspicions of her self-appointed watchdog, the postboy. She needed to catch the stage to London, and she needed to do it before Edmond Lawrence came to his senses and exposed her as a fraud. Unfortunately, she had not yet figured out how she was to get away from the posting inn, not with the postboy observing her every move, just waiting for her to make a false step so he could haul her to Squire Clegg and accuse her of thievery.

The innkeeper at the Ram, his wife, and the good doctor had all accepted Honor's fabrication that she and her husband were on their way to Abbingdon to stand vigil at the deathbed of Edmond's beloved grandfather. As well, they had not even questioned her story about the trunks being accidentally transferred to some other coach during travel.

The postboy, however, was made of sterner stuff. Young Davey may have tipped his white beaver hat politely and taken himself off to the stable, but his eyes had told Honor that he was not so easily fooled, that he would be watching her.

To Honor's everlasting gratitude, the young caddie who had lost control of the team had fled the little village before she and the injured man had arrived. Probably fearing that he would be held responsible for the passenger's injuries, the lad had taken the team and disappeared, presumably returning to the posting inn at Exeter. With the caddie gone, there was no one who could prove beyond doubt that Honor had not been in the post chaise the entire trip. Actually, no one but young Davey even questioned it, especially not after Honor began dispensing Edmond's considerable largesse to procure him a comfortable room.

But Honor's luck had not held, for the continued snowfall had made further travel inadvisable for a day or so, which meant the postboy would not be taking out any "Yellow Bounders." By the same token, the weather would keep Honor from catching the stagecoach to London. She would be obliged to remain at the inn until the roads cleared.

Her thoughts were interrupted by a muffled moan, and as she looked toward the plain, oak sleigh bed with its stack of thick quilts, Edmond began to toss about. Though his voice was hoarse, he began calling for someone named Avery to watch his flank.

"Must make it to the redoubt! Careful, lads."

Honor went over to the bed and tried to pull the covers back over his shoulders, but Edmond reacted as though she were trying to capture him, flailing his arms about in such a way that she jumped back to avoid being hit.

"The major is down," he muttered again. "Damned grapeshot! Help me get him . . ." The words became indistinct, and as they faded into occasional nonverbal sounds, the patient grew still.

Moving cautiously, Honor approached the bed again, this time keeping some distance between her and the sick man. He obviously believed he had returned to the war, and though she felt sympathy for him, she had no desire to figure as one of Napoleon's troops. Edmond Lawrence was a big man, taller than average, with broad shoulders and muscular arms, and his hands were of a size that could quite easily span her throat and choke the life from her body.

"Mrs. Lawrence," said a hushed voice from the doorway.

Honor jumped as though the exiled Napoleon himself had come through the door.

"Begging your pardon, I'm sure," the innkeeper's wife said.

"It is quite all right, Mrs. Trogdon. I fear you caught me woolgathering."

"It's worried you are, ma'am, and who's to wonder at it."

The plump, middle-aged woman stepped into the room and approached the foot of the bed. Her starched mobcap was slightly askew, and though her breathing was labored from the climb up to the second floor, the concern on her homely face was genuine.

"I came to tell you personal like," she said, regret in her voice, "that the old lady as has the room next to this one is staying another night. On account of the weather, don't you know. So, much as I would like to oblige you, ma'am, I ain't able to provide you with an additional room."

"But there must be another bedchamber! I cannot—" Honor stopped just in time, coming perilously close to informing the landlord's wife that she could not share a room with the man who was supposed to be her husband, not without being compromised. "Any room would do," she said. "It need not be on this floor."

"I'm right sorry to be disobliging, but there just ain't no room." She indicated the folded sheets she held over her arm. "But never you fear, ma'am, Mr. Trogdon is bringing up a cot for you, on account of I told him you wouldn't want to disturb Mr. Lawrence by trying to share his bed."

If a human face could burst into flame, Honor's would have done so at the notion of sharing a bed with a man, any man. It was bad enough that she was here in his room. If it ever became known that she had spent the night in a gentleman's bedchamber, she would be ruined. Unable to hide her embarrassment, she turned away so the woman could not see her face.

Misinterpreting the blush as the understandable modesty of a new bride, Mrs. Trogdon made clucking noises like a mother hen. "I know the ways of the quality," she said, "and I reckon sharing a room ain't what you're used to. But mayhap it'll just be for the one night." She smiled mischievously, then added with a wink, "Me and Johnny been slumbering back-to-back for near thirty years, and if the truth be told, I wouldn't have it any other way."

After setting the fresh sheets on top of a rather handsome oak chest of drawers stationed against the near wall, the woman gazed without embarrassment at the man who slept beneath the quilts, clothed in nothing but a flannel nightshirt lent to him by the innkeeper. "I'll tell you, ma'am, if I had me a fine looking man like your mister, wouldn't be any separate rooms needed, on account of I wouldn't let him out of my sight. And if you'll take a word of advice from a woman who's—"

"Mrs. Trogdon," called her husband from the stairs, "give us a hand here."

When the loquacious woman went to the door to help her husband with the cot, Honor breathed a sigh of relief, for she did not think she could have endured a lecture on the fulfillment of her wifely duties. Not without exposing herself as a charlatan.

While husband and wife positioned the small wooden bed that was little more than a collection of slats nailed to a narrow, rectangular frame, Edmond began to thrash about again, moaning and calling softly for someone to bring him his horse. Honor looked on helplessly, wishing she knew something that would ease his discomfort, but having had almost no experience attending the sick, she could think of nothing to do.

The doctor's only instructions had been to keep the patient warm and to give him barley water, but from the way Edmond was tossing about, only a fool would try to get water down his throat. As for keeping him warm, that, too, seemed ill-advised, for he was all but burning up.

Standing beside his bed, Honor could feel the heat emanating from his body. Cautiously, she touched her fingertips to his forehead. It was as she thought, he was giving off more warmth than the coals in the small grate beside the slipper chair.

The logical course of action or so it seemed to her, was to cool him off. Vaguely recalling some childhood malady she had suffered, Honor remembered her Uncle

Wesley sitting beside her bed, repeatedly bathing her face and arms with a cool cloth until her fever had broken. If her uncle thought it a good idea to cool a fevered brow, that was recommendation enough for Honor, for there was no wiser or kinder man alive than Wesley Coverdale.

Pleased to have thought of something constructive to do, Honor crossed to the far corner of the room where a washstand stood against the wall. She poured water from the plain crockery pitcher into the equally plain washbowl, then tossed a clean cloth into the bowl.

While the Trogdons continued to shift the cot from one spot to another on the uneven wooden floor, each one insisting they knew the exact place where all four wobbly legs would touch at once, Honor concentrated on her measured footsteps and the difficult task of walking without sloshing the contents of the bowl down the front of her gown. When she finally reached the bedside table, she breathed a sigh of relief, setting the washbowl down gently so as not to disturb the medicine in the glass.

Now, all that was left for her to do was to attend to the patient.

Although she felt decidedly ill at ease at the thought of performing such a personal task upon a virtual stranger—a man about whom she knew nothing but the name upon his calling card—she took a steadying breath, then wrung the excess water form the cloth. Hesitantly, she sat down on the edge of the bed and pressed the cloth to Edmond's heated forehead, being careful not to touch the bruised area that disappeared into his hairline. The instant she touched him, he seemed to relax.

Curiously, ministering to Edmond exercised a calming effect upon Honor as well, for her hands ceased to shake and her embarrassment soon disappeared. Each time the cloth lost its coolness, she got up, remoistened it, then returned to sit beside the patient and bathe his face, repeating the process again and again until he grew quiet as a babe.

At some point the Trogdons had completed their task and quit the room, but Honor was too busy concentrating on the man in the bed to notice their departure.

Gently, she smoothed the cloth across Edmond's temples, then continued down his whisker-shadowed cheeks to the area beneath his decidedly obstinate chin. An interesting face, she decided, touching the cloth to the strong column of his neck. Some might even say it was a handsome face.

Not that she cared for handsome men. To the contrary! She avoided them whenever possible. Her father had been handsome, with a ready smile and more charm than a good man would need or a bad man should have. Honor had learned early not to put her faith in such men. And with good reason. Her father had proved himself unworthy of the love of a devoted wife.

A second son, spoiled by indulgent parents, he had been encouraged from birth to believe he could take whatever he wanted and never mind the consequences. And when he beheld pretty Jenny Coverdale, a young woman not of his own social standing, he wanted her.

Despite Wesley Coverdale's entreaties to his sister not to marry the handsome soldier, Jenny paid him no heed, and for a short time she was happy with her dashing husband. At least she was happy until the letter arrived from Sir Harry and Lady Danforth. Her new father-in-law had learned of the mésalliance and refused to continue to pay his son's debts. With only his army pay, plus occasional handouts from Uncle Wesley, Lieutenant Danforth soon tired of his wife and child and disappeared, leaving Jenny ill and brokenhearted.

As well, it was because of another well-favored man that Honor had been forced to leave her home and her beloved uncle to seek employment as a governess.

Time and again she had rejected the unwanted attentions of Jerome Wade, Esquire. Suave, wealthy, and handsome, the tall, blond barrister with the cold gray eyes had been unwilling to believe that any woman would not be flattered by his attentions. Especially not a female who made her home with a solicitor whose yearly earnings equaled less than Wade expended on his elegantly tailored clothes.

When Honor refused Wade's offer of a carte blanche, going so far as to slap his face for the insult, he had become enraged, threatening to ruin her uncle if she did not reconsider the proposition. It was only when the threat failed to achieve its goal that more subtle methods were employed—hints of accidental injuries to family, to friends, to Honor herself.

Honor had not given real credence to the barrister's hints, not even when she had experienced an odd sensation that she was being watched when she left the house to complete such unexceptional errands as marketing or visiting the baker's shop. However, one morning she was forced to admit the foolishness of her disregard.

Discovering outside her door a beribboned basket, from whose handle hung an expensive card of invitation bearing Honor's name, she brought the gift inside the house. To her horror, when she lifted the expensive linen napkin that concealed the contents of the basket, she found the woven interior filled with a dozen dead rats. Around the neck of the largest of the rodents was a miniature noose bearing her uncle's name. Convinced now of Wade's mental instability, and of his unrelenting desire to have what he wanted, she had agreed to her uncle's plan and left for Devon the next day.

The memory brought renewed anger, anger that must have transmitted itself to her hands, for the patient groaned as if she had dealt too roughly with his throat. Realizing she had taken out her resentment upon the wrong man, Honor said, "Forgive me, sir," then sought to make amends by lightly pressing the cloth to Edmond's throat.

He grew still again, and Honor, thinking it might bring him further relief, decided to loosen the neck of his nightshirt. The front opening was secured by a simple set of tapes sewn into the narrow neck band, and when the innkeeper had dressed the patient, he had tied the tapes much too snugly.

The flannel shirt was banded across the top of the shoulders, then gathered on the band for extra fullness and added freedom of movement. As a result of that fullness, when Honor turned the quilt down to Edmond's waist and unfastened the tapes, the garment seemed to fall away on both sides, exposing a goodly portion of his chest, stopping only where the quilt restrained it.

Though aghast at what had happened, and fully aware that any woman with a shred of modesty would turn away immediately, Honor was unable to move. Her legs seemed to have forgotten their primary function, and her lungs had shut down entirely. As thought mesmerized, she stared at the exposed flesh.

Before that moment she had never seen a man without his shirt. Even so, she knew instinctively that Edmond's chest was a prime example of masculine beauty. It was broad and ridged with muscle; and in that area just above his heart, a tantalizing sprinkling of hair grew, silkier, yet darker than the hair upon his head.

Honor's own heart seemed to be beating against her rib cage, fighting to escape its bonds.

Several moments passed before she was able to force her trembling fingers to retie the tapes of the nightshirt and conceal Edmond's chest, and only then was she able to breathe again. Still none too calm, she yanked the quilt back up around his shoulders, then escaped to the other side of the room, putting as much distance as possible between her and the man in the bed.

Now it was *her* skin that felt warm—much too warm to allow her to sit beside the grate—so she stood at the window that looked out onto the snow-covered inn yard. Resting her heated forehead against the icy panes, she closed her eyes and tried to still her erratic breathing.

"I should not have touched him," she whispered. "I had no right."

Honesty compelled her to admit that it was a bit late to be deliberating that home truth. The long and short of it was that she should never have set foot inside the bedchamber. And she knew it! But she had been faced with a choice: Confess to having lied about being Mrs. Lawrence, and chance being arrested for theft; or stay with the injured man in what was a thoroughly compromising situation.

At the time it had seemed like no choice at all. Even now she could think of nothing she could have done differently. All she asked of the perverse fate that seemed to rule her destiny of late was that her Uncle Wesley never learn of her reprehensible behavior.

Thinking of her uncle brought Honor's thoughts once again to the stagecoach that would take her back to London. If only she could walk out of the inn this instant and climb aboard the coach. If that were somehow possible, she vowed she would not utter a single word of complaint about the trip, no matter how rough the ride, nor how many people they stuffed inside the vehicle, nor even how little time they allowed the passengers to refresh themselves at the coaching inns. Happily would she suffer those annoyances and more, if only she could leave before her deception was found out, or before some new catastrophe befell her.

A thrashing sound from across the room interrupted her dreams of escape, and though she looked toward the bed, she turned away immediately, heat once again invading her cheeks.

"Whatever happens," she said with some vehemence, "I must not—will not—go near that man again."

Some vows are easier spoken that kept.

Honor discovered the maxim to be all too true. She might have wished never to go near Edmond again; she might even had sworn to all she held sacred that she would not. But time and circumstances have a way of forcing a person to recant even the most faithfully spoken promises.

Before that endless day and night were over, she had done more than go near him. To ease the steadily rising fever, she had bathed Edmond repeatedly, all the while crooning softly to him, and replacing the covers he kicked away every few minutes.

And during those times when the opium-laced barley water failed to stop the visions of past battles and fallen comrades—visions that held him in their clutches, taunting him and making him cry out and attempt to escape both the memories and the bed—she had wrestled with him until he grew calm.

By Tuesday morning, when Mr. Trogdon came to the room "to do for the gentleman" so Honor could go belowstairs to partake of a well-deserved breakfast, she was almost as acquainted with Edmond's body as she was with her own.

And still the snow came. All through the night and morning, it never once let up enough to permit travel in or out of the village. Not that it mattered now, for even if the roads had been clear, Honor would not have carried out her plans to flee. Her conscience would not have allowed her to leave Edmond. Not while he was still so sick.

At some point during the early morning hours, when the inn had been hushed with the silence of sleeping humanity, and the sky had been that dark blue that is the first promise of the day, Honor had made a pledge to Edmond Lawrence. A commitment she would not break.

She had been sitting in the slipper chair near the dying fire, a quilt wrapped around her for warmth, when she heard Edmond mumble something. Thinking he spoke to her, she pushed the cover aside and went over to the bed to see what he wanted. When she was beside him, however, she realized he had spoken not to her but to someone in his dreams.

"No more," he muttered, his voice so raspy she had to listen carefully to understand the words. "I will not kill again. Do not ask it of me."

"No, sir," she whispered, closing her eyes against the shock of hearing such a tormented entreaty. "I shall ask nothing of you but that you try to sleep."

"No more," he repeated.

"Shh," she said, taking his hand between hers and stroking it softly, hoping the touch of another human might comfort him. "You may rest easy, sir, for the war is over. There will be no more killing and being killed."

"So many dead. George and Harry. Even Franklin. Gone. All gone."

His anguish wrung Honor's heart, and as she continued to hold his hand, tears trickled from the outer corners of his eyes, slipping unheeded past his temples to disappear into his thick, tousled hair.

"God forgive us," he whispered.

"Amen," she said.

Bending close, she used the pad of her thumb to brush away his tears. Then, reluctant to abandon him to his sad memories, she stayed beside the bed until he slept again. It was while she stood thus that she made her pledge to him—a promise not to leave him to the mercy of strangers. No matter how much she wished to escape, she would stay until Edmond was himself again.

"It's fagged out you're looking," the innkeeper's wife said the moment she saw Honor standing in the doorway of the breakfast parlor. "With them dark circles under your eyes, I misdoubt you slept so much as a wink last night."

"And a good morning to you, too, Mrs. Trogdon."

Missing the sarcasm, the woman curtsied. "Thank you, ma'am. You'll be wanting something nourishing, or I miss my guess, so if you please, come this way."

Honor stepped inside the front room, which did double duty as breakfast parlor at the Ram, then followed Shirley Trogdon across a garish Turkey rug to one of the four cloth-covered tables. At the table nearest the fireplace, two middle-aged ladies sat conversing softly, while on the opposite side of the room, next to the window, a family of three ate their meal without exchanging so much as a word. In the corner an elderly gentleman sat in a chintz-covered wing chair, a cup of tea in one hand and a copy of *The Gentleman's Magazine* in the other.

None of the guests acknowledged Honor's entrance, but she could not blame them for choosing not to notice her. Other than looking fagged out, as Mrs. Trogdon had so kindly pointed out, she still wore the same maroon dress she had donned the morning before, and it was now far from fresh.

"I've saved this place for you," Mrs. Trogdon said, indicating a small table where a pewter-covered plate had been set on the crisp white linen cloth.

Taking her seat, Honor spread her napkin across her lap, then inhaled appreciatively as Mr. Trogdon removed the pewter cover from a plate of basted eggs and thinly sliced ham. "Mm. That smells delicious."

"Well, I hope it may be. To tell the truth, ma'am, I haven't had a spare moment to sample my own cooking. What with the inn being so full, and all, I don't know if I'm standing on my head or my feet."

She stuffed her work-roughened hands into the pockets of her white apron, then continued her monologue. "With only the one girl to help me, it's all I can do to see the food is cooked and the crockery scrubbed for the next meal. And I tell you something else, ma'am, it's a real blessing your poor mister wasn't traveling alone. I don't know what we would have done with him, and that's a fact, and *I* certainly haven't got time to be taking care of a sick gentleman."

Muttering some kind of response, Honor busied herself with pouring a cup of hot, steaming tea from a daisy-patterned teapot. While she drank thirstily of the fragrant liquid, the innkeeper's harried wife replaced the woven cozy over the pot and continued her monologue.

"Like I was telling Johnny last night," she said, "it's a lucky thing for Mr. Lawrence that he wasn't alone when he fell ill. 'Johnny,' I said, 'if you ask me, the smartest thing Mr. Lawrence ever did was to get himself a wife.' "

As far as Honor was concerned, the smartest thing she did was take a turn around the small inn. Hoping for nothing more than a bit of exercise, she was elated to discover, in the far corner of the public room, an item that would solve at least one of her immediate problems—her need for privacy.

Shoved against the wall, dusty and forgotten, was an old-fashioned bi-fold dressing screen. With visions of removing her crumpled dress and having a good wash, Honor hurried across the room to investigate the treasure.

The frame of the screen was fashioned of hazel wood, its two panels a white silken fabric. Painted upon the panels was an unimaginative pastoral scene depicting rolling green hills and a dozen vacuous-looking sheep, all languishing beneath myriads of puffy white clouds. The insipid painting notwithstanding, Honor was pleased to discover that the fabric contained no tears or breaks, and that the frame was still capable of standing without toppling over.

Fearful lest she be accused of theft a second time, she returned the item to the corner where she found it, then dusted off her fingers and went upstairs to the bedchamber to ask Mr. Trogdon if he would have someone bring the screen up to her.

"The screen, missus?" The innkeeper's face looked almost as blank as those of the painted sheep. "Begging your pardon, I'm sure, but what would anyone be a-wanting with that old thing?"

Thinking fast, Honor said, "To keep the candlelight from shining in Mr. Lawrence's eyes. It disturbed him last night."

The man pondered the statement for a moment before nodding his head. "Right, then. I'll see the screen is dusted off afore it's brought up."

Edmond's head ached frightfully, as though someone had stuffed it full of cotton wool and used it for a cricket ball. In addition, his eyelids felt as though they weighed at least a stone each, much too heavy to lift. And yet, he wanted desperately to open his eyes. He wanted to wake up; to call to Crispin to bring him a soothing drink.

He did none of those things, however. To do so required more energy than he possessed, so he drifted back into that black chasm from which he had come.

When he resurfaced again, he knew it was much later. It was nighttime though how he knew when he still had not opened his eyes, he could not say. Perhaps it was the quiet of the room—that hushed stillness that comes only late at night. Or perhaps it . . .

What was that?

He'd heard something. What was it? Concentration was difficult with the chasm still holding him in its grasp, pulling him back, refusing to set him completely free. It reminded him of the marshes of the Peninsular, where he and his men had trudged through mire so deep it had come up to their thighs; mud that sucked them in and held them fast, as if it were sympathetic to Napoleon's cause and wished to detain his pursuers.

There it was again. That sound.

It was water. Yes, he thought, inordinately pleased to have solved the riddle. It was water being poured into something.

Slowly, and with great effort, Edmond opened his eyes. At first his vision was blurred, out of focus, and even when it sharpened and objects became more distinct, his bedchamber seemed odd, somehow. The dresser was on the wrong wall. And where was the reading stand that had belonged to his father? Had Crispin moved it? No. The valet knew better than to touch that stand. It was the only personal item Edmond had left of his father's.

Edmond fought the desire to close his eyes and drift away. It was all very confusing when nothing was the way it should be.

That screen in the corner. I never used to have a screen.

A light shone behind the screen, and he concentrated on that light. Was it a brace of candles? A small Argand lamp? Whatever its source, the brightness was diffused by the colors on the silk panels.

There were patches of green. And above the green it was white. White and puffy, like clouds. And something else. Dark, like a shadow.

It was a shadow. It moved, and for a moment Edmond thought it must be Crispin. But then there was the sound of water splashing in a bowl, and the shadow turned to the side, revealing a body in profile—a body that was delicately shaped and much too curvaceous to belong to the valet. A slender, graceful arm was raised, then moments later lowered, and the splashing sound came again, as though the shadow figure was bathing.

Marguerite? Was he at the little rented house on Clipstone Street?

No. That could not be, for he had not renewed the lease on the little house. Marguerite had become too greedy. She was under Lord Griffin's protection now, and he . . .

Edmond lost his train of thought, and though he struggled to recapture it, the exertion was too taxing and he was tired. So very tired. Even the lovely shadow seemed to be fading. Fading. Fading . . .

The next time Edmond opened his eyes, it was morning, and radiant, clear light shown through a window at the opposite side of the room, casting a rectangle of brightness on the uncarpeted oak floor and sending a shard of pain through his throbbing head. From outside the window came the shout of a driver attempting to halt carriage horses, followed only moments later by the unmistakable jingle of bridles as the animals were unhitched.

" 'Ere, Thomas," someone yelled from below the window, "step lively there, lad. We've not got all day. These 'ere 'orses be wanting their oats."

Whatever the lad's response to the order, Edmond failed to hear it, for his attention was claimed by a knock at the door. He wanted to bid whoever was outside to come in, but swallowing was difficult and speaking impossible. Before he had time to wonder how he was to make his wishes known, someone else spoke the words for him.

"Come in," called a soft voice from somewhere out of his range of vision.

It was a young woman's voice, soft and refined. And though Edmond could not identify it, there was something familiar about it, something that made him think he should be able to recognize its owner.

When the door opened, a plump woman in an apron and mobcap entered the room. A servant of some kind, she carried a maroon kerseymere dress over her arm. "Here you are, ma'am. As nice a job of brushing and pressing as you're like to see this side of London, even if I do say so myself."

"It looks wonderful," the voice said. "Thank you so much, Mrs. Trogdon."

The woman bobbed a curtsy, then walked around the dresser to the four pegs affixed along the wall, where she hung the garment between a brown wool redingote and a greatcoat Edmond recognized as his. As she turned from the task, she gave him a cursory glance that quickly became a second, more thorough inspection. With the second look her eyes grew wide with surprise.

"Well, now, sir," she said, a smile improving her plain, round face, "It's time you were returning to the land of the living. A fair long sleep you've had, and that's a fact."

When he would have asked her who she was, and where the deuce *he* was, she stopped his painful attempts at speech by turning toward the far end of the room.

"Ma'am," she said, "you'll want to see this, I'm thinking."

"What is it?" asked the still faceless voice. "Is Mr. Lawrence worse?"

"No, ma'am. If I was to venture an opinion, I'd say he was much improved. But come see for yourself. You'll be pleased to know that your husband is awake at last."

Chapter 3

*H*usband!

Edmond stared at the servant to see if she was in jest. Unfortunately, she had turned toward the bottom of the room and he could no longer see her face.

"Awake?" The voice sounded breathy, almost frightened. "But it is too soon! Are . . . are you certain?"

"Got his eyes open, leastways. But you'll want to come see him for yourself, Mrs. Lawrence."

Devil take it! There was no Mrs. Lawrence. His mother was Lady Frome now, and Edmond certainly had not bestowed the name upon any of the chits who pursued him so aggressively during their London seasons.

What kind of game was being played here? And who the deuce was playing it? The woman at the bottom of the room, obviously, but was the servant merely a dupe, or were the two of them in it together? And what on earth made either of them believe they could get away with their little ploy?

Money was involved, of course. There could be no other reason for a pretended marriage. Somehow—he could not quite remember the particulars—he had fallen into the clutches of a schemer, a vixen who thought she could separate him from a few thousand pounds. He would soon disabuse her of that notion. Although he possessed a quite comfortable fortune and could easily stand the nonsense, he would not do so, for if there was one thing he despised, it was a person without principles.

Determined to show her that he was no Johnny Raw to be diddled by a couple of females, Edmond reached for the covers, intending to toss them aside and jump to his feet.

Taller than average and physically fit, he had discovered years ago that his presence alone was enough to dissuade reckless young jackanapes from trying his patience. And though it was his usual practice to tread softly with women, lest his size frighten them, a good scare might be exactly what was called for in this instance. Perhaps it might convince these two to give over whatever nefarious scheme they had concocted.

Unfortunately, when he lifted his hand, it felt heavy as a cannonball, and totally unwilling to respond to the orders given it by his mind. As for jumping to his feet, he could not even sit up. He was as weak as a kitten, with reflexes so sluggish he had to wonder if he had been drugged.

Damnation! Drugs. That would explain the strange dreams, and why the inside of his mouth felt like a wool sock, not to mention the dull throbbing in the front of his skull. But perhaps his being drugged was a good sign. If the women felt obliged to render him incapable of moving about, that might mean there were no men involved, no strong-armed bruiser Edmond would need to subdue to escape. Cheered by that thought, and hoping to discover more about his situation, he chose the better part of valor and ceased the struggle to get up.

"You just lie still, sir," the servant said, "and let me straighten those covers. Once we have you fixed up, I'll go down to the kitchen, and sooner than you can say, 'Bob's your uncle,' I'll be back with a nice cup of tea. You'll like that, I'm sure. Meanwhile," she said, giggling like a schoolroom chit, "I know Mrs. Lawrence is wishing me anyplace but here, for you newlyweds will be wanting a moment alone."

Edmond frowned. If the so-called Mrs. Lawrence was indeed desirous of that private moment with her new husband, she was taking her own sweet time about putting in an appearance. For his part, he longed to see the woman, to observe for himself just what he was up against—a beautiful Circe, no doubt. Unfortunately, so far she remained nothing more than a mysterious voice in the far corner.

The servant straightened the quilts and fluffed the pillows until Edmond thought he would go mad with the unwanted attention. Finally, after smothering another giggle behind her hand, she bobbed a curtsy and left the room.

For a time the bedchamber was quiet, with only the clear jingle-jangle sounds of horses being hitched to a carriage outside, and the muffled sound of voices somewhere inside the house. Still, the illusive female remained across the room. When Edmond despaired of ever getting a look at her, she suddenly appeared at the foot of the bed, her steps surprisingly noiseless upon the wooden floor.

He could only stare at the woman who stood before him, for she was not at all what he had expected. Here was no Circe. Neither her demeanor nor her attire were those of a seasoned seductress. Far from offering him honeyed smiles or provocative glances, she was reserved, keeping her eyes downcast, almost as if modesty—or embarrassment—compelled her to do so.

To Edmond's further surprise, the woman had wrapped a quilt around her like a cloak and was holding the ends together firmly with one hand, as though a chill wind blew through the room.

Cocooned within the thick quilt, her figure was well concealed. However, he suspected he had already been afforded a glimpse of her charms, for surely she was the source of the shadow behind the screen last evening, the female performing her ablutions.

When she came around to stand beside the bed, giving Edmond his first opportunity to observe her from head to toe, he discovered that in addition to her unusual ensemble she wore a decidedly unprovocative pair of blue and yellow carpet slippers. Also, around her ankles six or eight inches of chaste white lawn showed beneath the makeshift wrapper. *A nightrail? Had she slept here? In this room? In this bed?*

Quickly, he glanced at her face, as if expecting to find a look of wantonness there, but he detected nothing save that same reserve. He did not know what to think of this anomaly who was his supposed wife.

Edmond guessed her age to be about four and twenty. Blessed with a soft, clear complexion and a delicately sculpted face, she was pleasant-looking rather than pretty. The thing that held him spellbound was her hair. A brown so dark it was almost black, and straight as the blade of a fine sword, the hair spilled down her back like layer upon layer of lustrous silk.

A good thing for Edmond that his hand was too heavy to obey the impulse, for he was tempted to reach out and catch that dark silk between his fingers to test its texture.

Since he was in no danger of acting upon that temptation, he took his time looking her over, scrutinizing her from the extraordinary hair down to the mundane footwear. His perusal completed, he was about to demand an explanation for her using his name, when her black lashes swept up and she looked at him for the first time, rendering him speechless.

All else was forgotten as eyes the clear blue of a mountain lake beneath a cloudless sky gazed directly into his. And while he stared into those remarkable eyes with their thick sooty lashes and gracefully arched brows, Edmond wondered how he ever could have thought her merely pleasant-looking.

The woman was beautiful.

"You will be wondering where you are," she said, her softly spoken words breaking the spell she had cast upon him. "And though you must have a million questions, I am persuaded it would be best for your poor throat if you did not try to speak just yet."

Though her words exhibited just the right amount of concern, Edmond suspected that his throat was not the thing she most wished to spare. The woman did not want to be questioned, and in his present condition there was little he could do to force answers from her. Deciding that keeping his ears open might prove more beneficial than speech, he nodded his head, encouraging her to tell him what she would.

"First of all," she said, "You are in Devon, at a posting inn situated in a little village called Lower Chidderton."

Devon! Edmond kept his reactions to himself, not wanting to reveal his disbelief. He had not judged the woman to be a fool, but she must be if she thought to convince him that he was so far from London.

"There was an accident," she continued. "Snow and ice made the roads treacherous, causing your chaise to skid and tip over. And though you sustained only minor injuries, you were in no condition to continue your journey to Abbingdon."

He only just stopped himself from smiling. *You slipped up there, my beauty, for why the devil would any man want to go to a place called Abbingdon?*

Giving it a second thought, however, the name sounded vaguely familiar. Something niggled at the back of Edmond's brain. Concentrationg for several moments, he finally remembered where he had heard that name before; his father's cousin, Sir Frederick Raleigh, owned an estate in Abbingdon.

No. That was not quite right. Cousin Frederick *used* to own an estate there. Yes, that was it. Sir Frederick was dead. It was *Edmond* who now owned the estate in Abbingdon.

"But the good doctor said the bruise on your forehead was but a trifle and should not plague you for long."

Edmond blinked. *What was she saying?* He returned his attention to the woman. He must keep his wits about him, not let his thoughts wander, for if he was to fit together the puzzle that was the past few hours of his life, he must have all the necessary pieces.

As if to show her that he was attending her words, he lifted his hand to his forehead and tested the tender spot at the edge of his hairline. Though he winced at his own careless exploration of the bruise, he had sustained enough such injuries in his life to be virtually unconcerned by one more.

What startled him was the discovery he made when he let his fingers slide from his forehead to the lower half of his face. Expecting an overnight shadowing of stubble upon his jaw and chin, he was shocked to find himself positively hirsute—a condition he had not experienced since his Peninsular days when he had been obliged to forgo shaving for long periods of time.

Clearly, his face had not seen a razor for a number of days, and the realization was unsettling, to say the least. For the first time since waking, Edmond felt a frisson of concern. Days? Suddenly, the puzzle appeared more complicated, the pieces more numerous. It was one thing not to recall a few hours, quite another to have lost whole days of one's life.

"What is," he muttered, the rawness of his throat forcing him to pause and swallow, "what day?"

"Today, do you mean?"

He nodded.

She answered primly, sounding rather like a governess imparting information to her pupil. "It is the year of our Lord, eighteen-hundred and nineteen, and the day is Wednesday, January thirteenth."

Edmond closed his eyes, not wanting to reveal to her the blow that seemingly innocent piece of information had dealt him. If today was Wednesday, what had become of Tuesday? And Monday? Or for that matter, what of Sunday? He racked his brain for a memory— anything he could associate with a particular day, a definite time. The only thing that came to mind was a recollection of Crispin honing his razor.

Crispin! At least Edmond remembered his valet Cecil Crispin. They were in his bedchamber, in his bachelor quarters at number twenty-seven Chesterfield Street, just down the way from Avery's digs. Freshly pressed evening clothes lay upon the bed, waiting to be donned. And on the far side of the room the valet stood at the mahogany washstand, his large hook nose in profile, his attention fixed upon the razor he whisked back and forth across the leather strap.

But when was that?

Crispin had been with him since Edmond resigned his commission in the "Light Bobs" and returned to London, his one ambition to forget the horrors of war and enjoy the uncncumbered life of a bachelor gentleman. The scene at the washstand could have occurred anytime during the last three years.

Edmond felt his brows knit in his attempt to remember. The woman must have seen the gesture and misinterpreted it, for she asked him if he was in pain.

"The doctor left a bottle of tincture of opium. You may have a drop if you need it."

So. He was correct. She had been drugging him. He opened his eyes to look at her, to see if she realized she had given herself away, but her countenance gave witness to nothing more than the concern she had expressed for his health.

"Normally," she said, "I do not approve of dosing, but your sleep was so troubled I feared you might injure yourself. It was the fever; it caused such distressing dreams."

What fever? Had he been ill?

"More than once you tried to quit your bed. I gave you the laudanum when I could no longer restrain you."

For some reason, uttering the word *restrain* caused crimson to creep up her lovely neck, tinting her creamy cheeks a rosy hue, and once again she lowered those sooty lashes so that Edmond could not see her eyes.

"I was ill?" he whispered. "And you took care of me?" When she nodded her assent, he asked rather sharply, "Who are you?"

He paid the price for his impulsive questions with a fit of coughing that threatened to leave his throat in shreds. When the woman offered him the barley water, he accepted it gratefully, allowing her to hold the half-filled glass to his lips while he drank thirstily.

It was only after he had drained the last drop of the soothing liquid, and was watching her struggle to readjust the quilt that was slipping from around her, that he remembered about the tincture of opium. Unfortunately, by that time it was too late; his body was already growing weightless, as though it might rise from the bed at any moment and float around the room. Conversely, his eyelids were so heavy he could no longer keep them open.

The last thing he heard before he drifted into oblivion was the woman's voice. It sounded strange, echoing, as though she were standing on a remote mountaintop, calling down into the valley below.

"Honor," she said.

Having forgotten his earlier question, he wondered why she should introduce a discussion of ethics at this time, but he was much too sleepy to give the subject any real consideration.

"Rest now," she said.

As she leaned forward to place his arm beneath the covers and tuck them snugly around his shoulders, a length of that dark silk that was her hair spilled over and touched his face. Instantly, she straightened, tossing the silken tresses back over her shoulder, but not before a hint of fresh, clean woman teased Edmond's nostrils. "Rest," she said again. "All will be well soon. I promise."

Edmond thought he heard her say, "Good-bye," but he could not be certain of it, for the drug had won at last. He was floating away.

For her part, Honor was not sure how much of last night's opium had remained in the glass of water she gave him, so she waited beside the bed until she was certain Edmond slept soundly. Convinced by his deep, rhythmic breathing that he would not soon awaken, she yanked the quilt from around her body and tossed it across the foot of the bed. Quickly, she stepped over to the pegs on the wall where, with trembling fingers, she lifted down the maroon kerseymere dress Mrs. Trogdon had brushed and pressed for her.

The questions had started. Of course, there would be many more once Edmond regained his strength enough to wonder how he had acquired a wife whose name and face were unknown to him. He would be justifiably angry—perhaps angry enough to insist that she be arrested—and Honor needed to get away now, while she still could.

Ten minutes behind the screen was enough time for her to remove her nightrail and don her drawers, shift, petticoat, dress, and guimpe. Admonishing herself not to rush so much that she grew careless, she perched on the edge of the slipper chair and pulled on her plain woolen stockings and her half boots.

Years of practice enabled her to brush her long, thick hair without the aid of a looking glass, then twist it into a knot and pin it atop her head. After affixing the little enamel watch to her collar, and checking in her reticule to make certain the borrowed five-pound note, along with her own guinea and six-pence, were still safely tucked inside her tan kid glove, she replaced her few personal items in the ancient leather valise, fetched her redingote from the peg on the wall, and tied on the brown velvet bonnet.

The last task she completed before quitting the room, and the one she found hardest to execute, was to retrieve Edmond's pocketbook from the dresser drawer where she had put it for safekeeping, and slip an itemized list inside, detailing the money expended on his behalf. At the bottom of the page were her vowels for the five pounds she had borrowed, an IOU that bore only her first name. She had been afraid to affix her full name, lest he send the authorities to apprehend her.

Pushing the pocketbook beneath Edmond's pillow, she took one last look at him. His color was better than it had been two days ago, and though he was in need of a shave, his angular face appeared relaxed, no longer tormented by dreams of war.

Honor had thought it an interesting face, but now she admitted rather grudgingly that it was also a handsome one. Not wishing to examine why that realization did not elicit its usual contemptuous reaction in her, she reached out and gently brushed a lock of coffee-colored hair from Edmond's forehead.

At her touch, he opened his eyes, revealing brown irises that were a perfect match for his hair, and for one frightening instant Honor thought she had dashed her own plans for escape. Fortunately, he gazed at her for mere seconds before his eyelids closed once again.

Remaining as still as a rabbit caught out in the open, she waited until Edmond's breathing returned to its rhythmic pattern. Not daring to delay a moment longer, she tiptoed over to the door, picked up her valise, and quietly left the room.

After having remained inside the inn for the better part of two days, Honor found the cold more biting than usual. It stung her eyes, burned her skin, and made her want to cough with each breath she took. Holding her handkerchief over her nose and mouth to help filter the lung-searing air, she walked to the edge of the inn yard, where a weathered wooden sign in the shape of a ram swung from the limb of a centuries-old oak tree.

Standing beneath the sign, Honor could see the entire village of Lower Chidderton, from the top of the high street to the bottom. In vain she tried to locate the coaching inn where she had been set down more than a month ago when she came to take up her post as Ivy Bascomb's governess.

It was odd how a heavy accumulation of snow could change the appearance of a village. This one seemed much smaller than she remembered it, and as she read the signs above each of the half-dozen shops, not one of them indicated the existence of a coaching inn. It was nowhere to be found. An absurdity, of course, for inns did not just up and walk away.

Afraid the suspicious postboy might come out of the stables and discover her, valise in hand, Honor left the inn yard and trudged through the snow to the shop nearest the Ram. It was a saddlery, and when she entered the pungent-smelling establishment and closed the heavy wooden door behind her, she found to her relief that there were no customers, only an old man sitting at a workbench. Dressed in thick corduroy breeches and a badly stained smock, the saddler wore a woolen cap upon his head, and his face was so dried and wrinkled it resembled the assortment of leather goods hanging from the wall behind the counter.

Looking up from the harness he held between the gnarled fingers of his left hand, he saluted Honor by touching his forehead with an awl he held in his right hand. "Something I can do for you, miss?"

Forcing a smile to her cold lips, she said, "Will you direct me to the coaching inn?"

"Well, now," the saddler said, slipping the tip of the

awl beneath his woolen cap to give his scalp a vigorous scratching. "I'm afeared I can't do that, miss. Glad to direct you to the posting inn, if you like. The Ram, it's called, and it be right next door. Couldn't miss it if you tried. But bain't no coaching inn in the village."

Honor blinked, wondering if the old man had accidentally pierced his brain with the punching tool. Either that, or he had worked too long among the smells of untanned hides and glue. Perhaps she should suggest he open a window for ventilation. "Of course there is a coaching inn. I cannot remember what it is called, but I was set down there when I traveled from London."

"Begging your pardon, I'm sure, miss, but bain't no stagecoach what passes through Upper Chidderton."

"But there is, I tell you. There must be, for I—"

Honor gasped as the realization of what the old man had said finally penetrated her own brain. "Upper Chidderton? Did you say *Upper*?"

"Yes, miss. Been called that since I was a lad. Since my pap were a lad, too, I reckon. Leastways—"

"But it cannot be! I am supposed to be in *Lower* Chidderton."

The old man *tsk-tsked*. "This is Upper Chidderton," he repeated, enunciating the words carefully, as if talking to one whose wits had gone lacking. "Lower Chidderton be eight miles due south."

Chapter 4

Honor caught hold of the counter with both hands and closed her eyes, as if by doing so she might shut out the truth of her situation. She was in the wrong village. Had been all along. Monday, when she left Bascomb Manor, she must have become disoriented by the heavy snow. When the road forked, she had chosen unwisely.

"Now what am I to do?" she said, not realizing she had spoken the question aloud. "I must catch the stagecoach to London."

"You shouldn't have come to Upper Chidderton," advised Job's comforter. "Bain't no stagecoach what passes through here."

"So you said before," Honor retorted, only just curbing a desire to yell epithets at the man. "Can you suggest a way for me to get to Lower Chidderton?"

The saddler pondered the question for a moment, making use of the awl to relieve an itch between his shoulder blades. "Reckon Gillis could give you a ride in his wagon when he goes over to fetch the mail."

Cheered by the possibility, Honor asked where she might find the wagoner.

"He be in Exeter, miss. Gillis always goes to Exeter of a Wednesday. Be back late Friday."

* * *

For the next hour Honor plodded her way through the ankle-deep mixture of snow and mud to enter each of the establishments in the village, from the saddlery down to the pig-killer's at the bottom of the high street. To her growing disappointment, no one had been able to suggest a way she might travel to Lower Chidderton that day.

Most of the shopkeepers, being suspicious of strangers, had not even listened to her words before shaking their heads in denial. And to add insult to anxiety, the wife of the draper had pursed her mouth as though she had eaten a green persimmon, then informed Honor in no uncertain terms that they wanted nothing to do with the goings-on of unescorted females.

With no other option available, Honor had returned to the Ram to see if anyone there might give her a ride. Knowing better than to approach the stables while the suspicious postboy was in residence, she had waited for the better part of an hour hidden behind the necessary, shivering with the cold, until young Davey had hitched up a post chaise and ridden off in an easterly direction.

The ostler, a sneaky-eyed fellow with an obvious aversion to soap and water, readily agreed to take her to Lower Chidderton. He would borrow the inn dogcart, he said, and take her anyplace she wished, just as soon as he finished his present job of currying and feeding the pair of grays that had come in with the last post chaise. And, of course, as soon as she presented him with a quid.

"A pound! You must be mad."

"Maybe so, missus. But I ain't the one as needs a ride to Lower Chidderton."

He had her there. He knew it, and she knew it. "But a

shilling should be sufficient for a drive of eight miles. To charge a person a pound is little better than highway robbery."

"Innerestin' you should mention robbery," he said, a smirk revealing gaps in his yellowed teeth. "Young Davey were tellin' me a story about a robbery just t'other day. Monday, it were. Summit about a female in a post chaise being caught red-handed robbin' a sick fella."

Honor strove to keep her facial expression composed, not wanting to reveal to the foul-smelling lout the sick churning within her stomach caused by his obvious threat. Highway robbery had begot blackmail, and she began to feel as if she had fallen into a hole—a hole that got deeper and deeper each time she tried to climb out.

Grudgingly, she ran the numbers through her head to see how she might pay the horrid man and still have the four pounds eighteen shillings needed for the coach ticket to London. Combining the money she borrowed from Edmond with the guinea given her by Uncle Wesley, plus the six-pence, she barely had enough for the ticket and the required tips.

Even if she gave the ostler only ten shillings to take her to the coaching inn, she would be obliged to forgo the tips for the coachman and the guard. Every fifty miles the coachmen expected at least two shillings, and tipping the double by ignoring the driver's outstretched hand was to court disaster. Honor had heard of some pretty nasty tricks being played on clutch-fisted travelers.

"Ten shillings," she countered. "That is the best I can do."

The ostler gave the horse's shank one last stroke, then tossed the currycomb onto a long, thin trestle table in the middle of the stable. "Your best ain't good enough, missus. You want to go to Lower Chidderton, it'll cost you a quid."

Unable to talk the wretched man into reducing his price, Honor debated the possibility of going back to the high street to see if one of the shopkeepers would lend her a few pounds on the little enamel watch she always wore. However, after giving it due consideration, she decided she could not part with the timepiece. Her mother had worn the watch every day of her life, and Honor would not give it into someone else's keeping, even for a short time. Of course, that left her with no choice but to return to the inn room and borrow another pound from Edmond's pocketbook.

Once again Edmond was awakened by a rap at the door. This time, however, he waited in vain for a voice from the far corner of the room to bid the person come in. There was only silence. After several moments, when the knock sounded again, he cleared his throat and called, "Enter."

"Well, sir, I see you are awake again. And looking much more the thing, if you'll pardon me saying so."

The serving woman—Mrs. Trogdon, the other one had called her—bustled into the room. There was a smile on her face, and in her hands she carried a small woven tray filled with dishes from which emanated the most tantalizing aromas Edmond had ever smelled. Pushing the door shut with her ample backside, she set the tray on the dresser, then approached the bed.

After looking around the room as though expecting to discover the other woman sitting quietly in some corner, she said, "Your wife not here?"

"My wife is definitely not here," Edmond whispered, the irony of the words lost upon his listener.

"That is too bad, on account of I was wishful of telling Mrs. Lawrence that the room next to this one has come available, in case she still wants that extra bedroom. I reckoned on telling her when she come down for breakfast, only she never came. When the morning wore on and I didn't see her, I took it upon myself to bring up a pot of tea and some sandwiches for her.

"And for you, sir," she added with a smile, "I've brought as nice a broth as you'll have tasted anywhere, if I do say so as shouldn't. Full of chicken and celery, it is, and guaranteed to heal what ails a body, putting him back on his feet and fine as five-pence in no time."

Without asking permission to do so, she picked up a quilt that had been tossed haphazardly across the foot of his bed; then after folding it lengthwise and rolling it into a bolster, she shoved it beneath Edmond's pillow, forcing him into a sitting position. There was a soft plop, as though something had fallen to the floor on the far side of the bed, next to the wall, but Edmond was in no shape to investigate. The room had begun to spin dangerously.

Thankfully, by the time the servant retrieved the tray and returned to set it across Edmond's lap, he had regained his equilibrium. When she lifted the pewter cover from the bowl, fragrant steam wafted up to his nose, causing his mouth to water and making him forget everything except the gnawing in his stomach. A situation not to be marveled at, for he had not eaten since Saturday morning.

Saturday morning. Yes! He remembered that. Remembered it clearly.

Crispin had served him a breakfast of soft boiled eggs and a filet of sole innocent of creams or sauces—just the way he liked it. Yet he had eaten sparingly, having felt decidedly down-pin since arising from his bed.

He also remembered Simon Avery coming around to his rooms some time after eleven, wearing a new coat. "I had it from Weston only yesterday," his friend had said, adjusting the lapels of the dark green coat that fit his slim person like a glove. "What think you of it?"

"Well cut," Edmond said. "I daresay all the young ladies will be giving you the eye."

"Naturally," agreed his friend with a wink.

Edmond had very nearly choked on his coffee. "Do try for a little modesty, my dear Avery. Believe me, it is the mark of a true gentleman."

Avery's rejoinder was decidedly ungentlemanlike and alluded to pots calling kettles black. "At any rate, it was you who introduced the subject of young ladies. I merely agreed that they would notice my new finery."

"And you are right, of course. Though why it should be so, I am sure I do not know. Only let a fellow have yellow hair and a pleasing face, and every foolish chit in London will throw herself in his path."

"Ho! Foolish, is it? And I suppose that was an assembly of scholars surrounding you the other day at the Pelham's alfresco party when you won the archery contest. *Oh, Mr. Lawrence,*" he mimicked in a falsetto voice, "*you are sooo big and strong.*"

Edmond clearly recalled having offered to toss his childhood friend through the front window.

"Sugar, sir?" Mrs. Trogdon asked, bringing his thoughts back to the present.

Edmond shook his head. Vastly relieved to have recollected parts of the past Saturday, he lifted the cup she had filled with tea and drank thirstily of the mahogany-colored brew.

"Eat up, sir, now do," she said, "for you'll need your strength if you and Mrs. Lawrence are to continue your journey to Abbingdon. Not but what you're sure to be too late for the funeral. When you didn't arrive on time, most likely your relatives buried the old gentleman as scheduled."

Edmond stared at the servant, unsure where she had got her information about a funeral at Abbingdon, but quite certain he possessed only one relative, and that one his mother. And anyone who knew his mother and her husband, Lord Frome, knew the pair never set foot in any but the most select country homes and the truly fashionable watering places.

"The broth, sir," Mrs. Trogdon prompted.

Like a sentry guarding his post, she stood with folded arms and watched until Edmond took the first few spoonfuls of broth. When he nodded his satisfaction, she beamed as though he had praised her to the heavens.

"Anything else I can do for you before I go, Mr. Lawrence?"

Once again he shook his head, and was thankful when she stopped fussing over him and quit the room. He needed quiet in which to think. To remember.

Abbingdon. What was it about the place? He had a feeling there was something he needed to know about it. Something important. Avery had mentioned it when he stopped by Saturday morning, and the subject had come up again when they dined together that evening. Yes. They had dined together; Edmond recalled both the meal and his friend's good-natured teasing.

"Must enjoy your company while I may," Avery had said, "for sooner or later you will be obliged to give in and journey to Devon."

"Better later than sooner," Edmond had replied.

"I understand perfectly, old boy, but you cannot ignore Lady Raleigh's letters of invitation forever. And once the widow and her daughter clap eyes on you, I would not wager a farthing on your being able to evade parson's mousetrap. Depend upon it, if the chit is not lovely enough to attract your notice, the mother will have devised some plan for compromising you into a proposal. The rest of us poor bachelors will probably never see you again."

That was it! That was the reason he had delayed going to claim his new estate. His cousin, Frederick, had remarried just prior to his demise, and his widow had a marriageable daughter. From Lady Raleigh's letters, it was clear she believed that because the property was entailed in Edmond's favor, she had a claim upon him for her daughter.

As to why, or how, he had come to be on the road, bound for Abbingdon and a matchmaking mama, Edmond could not even guess. No more than he could fathom how he had met the new Mrs. Lawrence.

Not that he believed for so much as an instant that he had wed anyone. He might recall nothing of Sunday, Monday, and Tuesday, but he remembered Saturday well enough, and this was only Wednesday. Three days missing. Hardly time enough to meet and marry a perfect stranger. And of one fact he was absolutely certain; he had never met the woman before in his life.

While he considered possible means of exposing the spurious bride for the fraud she was, he ate every drop of the delicious broth, as well as one of the cold beef sandwiches intended for his supposed wife.

By the time he had finished off the meal and half the pot of tea, he was feeling much more like himself. The pounding in his head was now little more than a dull throb, and he felt his strength returning by the minute. The condition of his throat still left much to be desired, but at least he could speak without experiencing a feeling reminiscent of cat claws scratching up and down his gullet.

After setting the tray on the bedside table, he was contemplating taking an experimental turn around the room when he heard soft footfalls just outside the door. It was her. Though how he recognized her step he could not say. But thinking he might learn more if the woman was unaware of his partial recuperation, he yanked the folded quilt from behind his pillow, tossed it onto the floor, then lay back, closing his eyes as if he were asleep.

Honor stood outside the bedroom door, wishing she could be anywhere but here, and wishing she did not have to reenter Edmond's room. Especially not for the reason she meant to reenter it—to relieve him of more of his money.

Like ripples spreading outward from a pebble tossed into a stream, an uncanny sequence of ill-fortune seemed to have begun with Honor's dismissal from the Bascomb household. Or perhaps it started earlier, with Jerome Wade, Esquire, and his offer of a carte blanche. Who could say when the figurative pebble was tossed, but now she was about to cause another ripple, for she needed an additional sovereign to pay her way to Lower Chidderton.

She breathed deeply in hopes of relieving the tightness in her chest. It was a tightness born of shame. After this debacle she would never be able to look her uncle in the eyes again. And even worse, she wondered if she would ever be able to face herself.

She doubted it.

And there was also the matter of her immortal soul. She prayed she had not already forfeited it, for if the religious teachings of her childhood were accurate, being a little bit dishonest was as impossible as being a little in the family way; one either was honest or one was not. Though, for the life of her, Honor could not think how she might have avoided this latest predicament.

Slowly, she opened the bedchamber door, careful not to let it squeak and betray her presence. Her palms were moist and her mouth dry, and as she set her valise on the floor by the screen, then tiptoed across to the bed, she prayed she could complete her contemptible task quickly and be gone before Edmond stirred.

He lay very still. His eyes were closed, and his breathing was even, and though a tray on the bedside table gave evidence that someone had eaten a meal recently, she did not suspect for a moment that he might be deceiving her.

She hesitated, her hand outstretched, not wanting to touch him. Foolish beyond permission when she had touched him hundreds of times in the past two days. Still, those times had involved caring for another human being—a far cry from dipping into an injured man's traveling funds.

Forcing herself to the sticking point, she reached her hand beneath his pillow. The weight of his head rested upon her arm, so she moved cautiously lest she wake him. She had expected to touch the leather pocketbook immediately, but to her surprise, her fingers encountered only the bed linen. Not a little puzzled, she began to feel around more aggressively, growing careless in her search until very nearly all of her arm was beneath the pillow, her head so close to his she could feel the warmth of his breath upon her cheek.

Oh my God! The pocketbook was not there. She had placed it beneath the pillow before she left, and now it was gone. Almost a thousand pounds—someone else's thousand pounds—and she had lost it!

Gripped by panic, Honor was about to snatch the pillow from beneath the invalid's head when an unbelievably strong arm suddenly grasped her around the waist and yanked her down on top of the man's broad chest, knocking the breath from her lungs and the bonnet from her head. Rendered powerless by the sudden attack, she was unable to do more than gasp, and before she knew what he was about, Edmond rolled to his left, taking her along with him until she was on her back and he was looming above her.

While she clutched at the bonnet ribbons that were practically choking her, Edmond propped up on his elbow and stared down into her face. An angry light shone in his brown eyes—a beware-where-you-tread look that made Honor's heart lurch painfully in her chest. She felt the blood drain from her face.

"Y . . . you are awake," she said, despising herself for the quiver in her voice, and him for putting it there.

He made no reply, merely continued to stare at her, as if searching her eyes for clues to a mystery. If he found the answers he sought, he did not apprise her of the fact, but as the moments grew, a subtle change took place. The anger in his eyes subsided, replaced by an uncertainty that was masked almost immediately by a look of lazy amusement, and ever so slightly he relaxed his hold upon her.

"Where were you?" he whispered very close to her ear, the raspy quality of his voice sending shivers down her spine. "I missed you . . . sweet wife."

Chapter 5

Sweet wife?

If Honor had been frightened before, it was nothing to the alarm she felt when she heard those words. Heaven help her, for Edmond had regained his strength but not his memory, and he thought they were married!

As she lay there, a prisoner held fast by his powerful arm, he moistened his bottom lip with the tip of his tongue, then slowly brought his face down to hers, as if he had every intention of kissing her. Honor knew she must not let that happen. Somehow, she must stop him— now—this moment. For if he believed her to be his wife, he might be laboring under the delusion that he could take husbandly liberties with her.

She turned her face away at the last moment so that his lips brushed not her mouth but her cheek, and as though that had been his destination all along, he nipped at her earlobe. The slight pressure of his teeth sent a riot of sensations through her, making her heart beat so rapidly she wondered that he did not comment upon the noise.

"Mmm," he murmured, as with soft, gentle little kisses, he began to work his way back toward her mouth.

"Let me go!" she ordered, wishing her voice sounded less nervous.

"And why should I do that?" he asked, his lazy smile revealing strong, white teeth.

"Because I . . . we . . ."

He propped himself back up on his elbow, then removed his arm from her waist, letting his hand linger for a second on her hip. When she stiffened at the contact, he reached up to her neck and began untying the ribbons to her bonnet. "Because we what?" he whispered, slowly pulling away first one ribbon then the other, exposing her throat.

Honor's heart felt as though it had stopped beating, and it took a concerted effort for her to draw enough air into her lungs to speak. "Because we . . . we are crushing my best bonnet!"

Though it was the truth, as a deterrent to husbandly urges the excuse lacked authority. And yet, Edmond surprised her by rolling onto his back and placing his hands beneath his head, allowing her to move away unimpeded.

Not waiting to see if he would change his mind, Honor sat up and scooted off the bed, intending to get as far away from him as possible. However, while she was still in that small space between the bed and the wall, the toe of her boot kicked something soft and yielding. Instinctively, she glanced down, and there on the floor was Edmond's pocketbook.

Instantly, she bent to pick it up, too relieved to have found the missing thousand pounds to think of disguising her actions. "Thank God," she said, holding the leather against her breast as though it were a lost child come home at last.

For just a moment, she entertained the notion of concealing the pocketbook from its owner, perhaps slipping it inside her redingote. But the recollection of his strength, not to mention the way he had looked at her while he untied the bonnet ribbons, convinced her that hiding something on her person might not be altogether prudent.

When she stood, she discovered Edmond watching her, and though a muscle in his tightly clamped jaw twitched as if in anger, she had the strange fancy there was disappointment in his eyes.

"Is that mine?" he asked.

When she nodded, he held out his hand. She hesitated a fraction of a second, but as badly as she needed that sovereign, she knew there was no hope of getting it now. Resigned to the inevitable, she reached across the bed to lay the pocketbook in his palm.

Honor thought she had felt shame before, but even with everything that had happened to her in the past four days, nothing had prepared her for the humiliation of that moment. And there was nothing she could say in her own defense. From the look he gave her, it was clear Edmond Lawrence believed she was a thief. He was right, of course. She might call it a loan, but the truth of the matter was, borrowing without permission was stealing.

As she placed the pocketbook in his hand, Edmond watched the color drain from her face. He expected her to offer some kind of excuse, but to his surprise, she said nothing. She merely did as he asked, then walked across the room and disposed herself in a small slipper chair in the corner next to the fireplace.

Still as a statue, she rested her head against the back of the chair, her eyes closed, and the badly crushed bonnet on her lap. If it was not for the slight trembling of her bottom lip—the one betraying sign that she was not as calm as she appeared—Edmond might have thought her undismayed by having been caught with his money in her hands.

Damnation! If she wanted money, why did she not just come out and ask for it; other women had found him generous enough.

Of course, she was not like the women who had enjoyed his protection. She was different. Or perhaps *inexperienced* was the better word. It was not inconceivable that this was her first foray into the world of the adventuress, for when he had pulled her into his bed, he had read real fear in her eyes. Of that he was certain. It had been all he could do to stop himself from offering her an apology.

Then she found the pocketbook, and he realized why she had been rooting around beneath his pillow. Someone must have put his money there for safekeeping, and she had only just discovered its location. Or perhaps she had known it all along but had waited until she was ready to make a run for it before she filched the cash. The latter was more than likely, for she was dressed for the out-of-doors, and a small valise sat on the floor near the painted screen.

Whatever her intentions, he wanted to hear them from her lips. He had made enough assumptions about her; he wanted the truth. Was she the innocent she appeared, or merely a very clever doxy? He was about to demand an explanation when there came a soft knock at the door.

"Mr. Lawrence?" called a voice he was surprised to hear. "Sir. Are you in there?"

"Yes, Crispin," he answered. "Come in."

The spindly valet opened the door and hurried to his master's bedside, a look of concern on his usually undemonstrative face. "Sir, the landlord informed me that you are ill."

"Were," Edmond whispered. "I am now on the mend."

A look of skepticism showed in the servant's serious gray eyes, though he did not refute the statement. "I am pleased to hear it, sir. I was that worried when Mr. Avery came round Sunday afternoon to say you had hired a post chaise and set out for Devon. Not but what I thought it all a hum at first, Mr. Avery being three parts disguised, and me knowing full well you had not the least notion of journeying to Raleigh Park as long as her ladyship was in residence. However, when—"

"How did you find me?" he asked, interrupting the valet's tale before he revealed more than Edmond wished overheard by their audience.

"Purest good fortune, sir. I delayed in town only long enough to pack such clothing as I thought you might need and have the carriage brought round, then I followed the path of the post chaise all the way to Exeter. At each of the posting inns I asked if anyone had seen you, but no one was able to offer me the least information. Happily, just as I was preparing to driving away from the Golden Hind, in Exeter, a young caddie came riding into the stable yard, his horses winded and his clothing muddy and disheveled, as though he had ridden long and hard.

"Frightened nearly out of his senses, the lad kept jabbering about an accident on the road. To my regret, by the time I had the entire story from him, and had determined in my mind that the gentleman in the evening clothes could be none other than yourself, the weather had grown worse, and I was obliged to remain at the Hind. Two days I cooled my heels until the roads were open once again."

While Crispin related his story, Edmond watched the woman rise from the slipper chair and walk quietly to the screen where she bent to retrieve her valise. He let her get almost to the door before he spoke. "Where do you think you are going?"

The valet turned to look behind him. Shocked to discover another person in the room, he muttered something beneath his breath before returning his attention to his employer. Incredulity was writ plainly on his countenance.

Ignoring the man's astonishment, Edmond focused his entire attention upon the woman, who stood straight yet tense, as if held at pistol point. When she vouchsafed no reply to his inquiry, an uncomfortable silence seemed to permeate every corner of the room. He swallowed painfully. Though the exertion of so much talking was taking its toll on his gullet, he repeated his question.

She did not look at him, but stared directly at the door. "I am in need of a breath of air. I thought I—"

"Leave the valise," he ordered.

Her chin lifted fractionally, as if she meant to defy him, but after a time she dropped the bag and exited the room, her shoulders back, her head held high.

The door was still ajar when the valet found his voice. "I had no idea you were entertaining, sir. Please forgive me if I intruded."

"You quite mistake the matter, Crispin. I was not entertaining." Just before the door clicked shut, he said, "I should, however, have made you known to the new Mrs. Lawrence."

Honor heard his words and wanted to scream her denial through the thick door. *No. I am not your wife. It was but a little white lie, a falsehood meant to save me from calamity.*

But she did not scream. Instead, she leaned her forehead against the wooden frame, closing her eyes as if in hopes of obliterating the events of the last half hour. This could not be happening. She had fled her home to escape the machinations of one man only to find herself at the mercy of another, this one believing he had a legal right to seek her out.

Misfortune awaited her at every turn. Why could she not open her eyes and find herself snuggled beneath the covers in her tiny bedchamber at Uncle Wesley's rooms in Marylebone, a participant in nothing more substantial than a bad dream?

When the tall, thin servant had entered the room and begun his story, Honor had thought she might be able to tiptoe out undetected. She still had her coach fare, and after that heart-stopping tumble in the bed, wisdom dictated that she walk the eight miles to Lower Chidderton—crawl if necessary—rather than remain another hour at the inn. Furthermore, the walk, no matter how difficult, could not be more distressing than the look in Edmond's eyes when she had handed over his pocketbook.

But she had not made good her escape. Edmond had prevented it, ordering her to leave her valise. It had crossed Honor's mind to defy him and make a dash for it, but she doubted she would have gotten far. Even if he was still too weak to stop her personally, a circumstance she did not trust for a minute, he had only to order the servant to do so in his stead.

Now, without her valise and the money tucked inside it for safety, she could go nowhere. For the life of her, Honor could not decide which fate was worse: To be a thief in constant fear of being arrested, or to be a counterfeit wife with no way to escape her supposed husband.

For his part, Edmond wrestled with a dilemma of his own. Though he never meant to come to Devon, he was here now, little more than an hour's ride from Abbingdon, and it was foolish not to continue the trip. Yet how was he to claim his inheritance without laying himself open to the risk of becoming a tenant for life with the widow's marriageable daughter?

The chance of entrapment was real. Especially on a country estate where little wooded walks, isolated outbuildings, and secluded corridors abounded, offering numerous opportunities for compromising an innocent party. Though, in this instance, it was debatable to whom the term *innocent party* applied.

In all conscience Edmond could not banish the girl and her mother from their home. Not immediately, at least. Not until he discovered if his cousin had left them comfortably fixed financially. They were, after all, connected to the Lawrence family.

For months he had pondered the predicament, unable to formulate even one possible solution to the problem. Until today.

Edmond was not certain at what moment the idea had come to him, but at some point between the kiss that never happened and the woman's attempt to sneak out of the room, the notion had begun to take shape. It was a preposterous plan, of course, but it had been *her* idea to play his wife. *He* meant only to perpetuate the ruse for a time.

Besides, what had he to lose? His single status, actually, but only if he was found out. He must claim his inheritance, and what better, safer way to do so than in the company of a nice new wife.

She would lose nothing in the bargain. Edmond would see to that. In fact, if she played her part well, she stood to profit handsomely from nothing more onerous than a few days spent in the country. Once Lady Raleigh saw that he was already married, and agreed to remove herself and her daughter from the premises, his *wife* was free to go, the recipient of a generous reward and a ticket to the destination of her choice. No harm done to anyone.

Quite pleased with his strategy, Edmond tossed the covers back and sat up, bidding the valet see to the hiring of fresh horses for the berlin. "Then bring me my shaving gear and some fresh clothes, for I wish to continue on to Abbingdon. Within the hour."

Arguments concerning his employer's recent illness and the chancy nature of the weather were alike ignored, and within a very few minutes Crispin, still dazed from the information that Mr. Lawrence had chosen to marry in secret, exited the room to carry out his instructions.

"And, Crispin," Edmond called before the door was closed.

The man stuck his head back inside the room. "Yes, sir?"

"Take Mrs. Lawrence's valise with you. And see it is stowed inside the berlin, beneath the front seat. For safety's sake," he added.

When the valet looked as if he would question storing ordinary baggage in a place intended to conceal such valuables as milady's jewel case, Edmond tossed him the leather pocketbook. "Take this as well. Use whatever you need to settle my bill, then put the rest with the valise."

"I shall do as you say," Crispin replied, catching the missile and placing it inside his coat. "And if I should encounter Mrs. Lawrence, shall I relay any message to her?"

"Yes. Tell her that we leave within the hour, then order her a pot of tea and see she eats something."

"As you wish, sir."

"And, Crispin."

"Yes, sir?"

"Tell her not to leave the inn. Impress upon her that I do not wish to be obliged to send a rescue party after her."

What the valet thought of this unloverlike message from a newly married man, he was too well trained to say. With a simple nod of understanding, he left the room, hurried down the steps to the ground floor, then set about fulfilling his master's orders . . . to the letter.

"You are certain I cannot persuade you to make use of the rug?" Edmond asked, lifting the corner of the handsome fur-lined carriage blanket that lay on the opposite seat. "The wind is quite biting."

Honor shook her head and slipped even closer to the side of the well-sprung berlin, pretending to gaze out a window so frosted over that observing the passing view was impossible.

Repeating his observation regarding the wind, Edmond added, "I, on the other hand, do not bite at all."

Honor turned quickly to see what he meant by the remark, but the teasing light in his brown eyes convinced her that he was only trying to put her at her ease, a task he had undertaken almost from the first mile they traveled. Unfortunately, she was impervious to his attempts to beguile the tedium of the trip and had treated his courtesy with monosyllabic responses verging on rebuff.

It was impotent anger that made her act with a want of common civility. But how could she behave otherwise, when she had lost all control of her own destiny? Edmond had her money—never mind that five pounds of it was rightfully his—and until she had it back in her possession, she could do nothing but go along with his decree.

And yet, honesty forced her to admit that she had no basis for holding *him* responsible for her being in this predicament. After all, it was *she* who had invented the story of their marriage. *She* who had stolen from him and would have to confess the whole and bear the consequences if he should elect to seek his husbandly rights.

Edmond Lawrence was totally blameless for this new debacle. And though he appeared relaxed, as if he were in complete control of the situation, she knew he must be beside himself trying to remember an event that never happened. Not that he had asked so much as one question. During the hour or so they had been traveling, he had not even broached the subject of their marriage.

And that, too, made her uneasy. Where were all the questions that must be making him anxious? Why had he not used this time to quiz her? He struck her as a very intelligent man; moreover, a man who led rather than followed. Surely, such a person would not accept her word alone as unassailable proof of their union.

It was all very unsettling.

Nor did it help her anger that he was making the best of the situation while she behaved churlishly. Feeling at a disadvantage, she remarked rather sarcastically, "I collect, sir, that you must be wishing me to the antipodes."

"On the contrary, ma'am. You may believe me when I

tell you that I would wish you no other place at this moment than by my side."

His words had an ironic ring to them, but when Honor searched his face to see if he was in earnest, all she detected was a rather inscrutable smile—a smile that was dispelled immediately by that easy manner she was coming to associate with him.

"What I do wish," he said, "is to know your name."

After steeling herself for an hour to face a barrage of difficult questions, this simple request took her by surprise. "I already told you my name," she blurted out.

The smile he turned upon her was apologetic, yet at the same time coaxing. And Honor had a fleeting suspicion that he was practiced in the art of persuading women to do as he wished.

"I fear my memory has become rather selective these past few days," he said. "There is so much that I am unable to remember clearly."

"Of course," she replied, her voice contrite. "I ask your pardon, sir. My name is Honoria, but I choose to be called Honor."

Honor. Edmond concentrated for a moment, recalling that time just after he had drunk the laudanum this morning. He had thought she was introducing the subject of ethics, when she had, in fact, told him her name. "Ah, yes. I remember now. And do *I* choose to call you Honor?"

She blushed rather prettily. "You . . . you do."

"Quite right," he said. "And you, of course, call me Edmond."

She made no reply, but studied her hands as they rested on her lap, the fingers laced together so tightly Edmond wondered that she did not cry out in pain. Using her discomfort to his advantage, he chose that moment to relay to her the fabrication he had decided best to tell the ladies at Raleigh Park.

"While we are on the subject of my faulty memory, there is something I would ask of you."

She raised those thick sooty lashes, pinning him with her unbelievably blue eyes, and for an instant he lost his train of thought.

"Ask?" she said, her voice just above a whisper.

"Tell, actually," he replied, calling himself to task for allowing a pair of lovely eyes to distract him from his purpose. "It concerns my reason for visiting Abbingdon. I have only recently inherited an estate outside the town, and—"

He stopped, shaking his head as though unable to believe his own stupidity. "Just listen to me. How foolish to apprise you of something you must already know. As though you, and not I, were the one with holes in their story. Surely, I told you of my inheritance prior to our marriage. Did I not?"

Color stained her cheeks, and she mumbled something that could have been anything from an affirmative reply to a prayer sent up to heaven.

"What I may not have mentioned is that two ladies presently reside at the Park—the widow of my cousin and the widow's daughter from a previous marriage. I tell you this so that you will be prepared, for I would not be at all surprised if the ladies are quite astounded to meet you. In fact, they may exhibit an extraordinary degree of curiosity about you and about our marriage."

At this news, his "bride's" face lost its color altogether.

"I would prefer," he continued, "that no one else know of my memory lapse. That being so, you will oblige me by answering all questions concerning the particulars of how we met, as well as any inquiry about our wedding, by stating that you and I have agreed to keep the entire interlude quite private between us."

"But no female would accept such a Banbury tale. The ladies will think—"

"What they think is of no consequence."

"But—"

"As for me, I will ask no questions of you."

Honor could not believe her ears. "No questions? None? But surely—"

"None whatsoever. I believe it would be best if I regain my memory unaided, and at my own pace."

While she stared at him, totally unable to credit his words, Edmond discovered an infinitesimal spot of dust upon the sleeve of his greatcoat and busied himself trying to flick it away.

"Also," he added, still concentrating upon the sleeve, "until such time as I recall every wonderful detail of our romance, as well as that mystical emotion that made us believe we might enjoy spending the rest of our lives together, I think it best that we eschew the, shall we say, more *private* moments enjoyed by husband and wife."

He glanced at her from the corner of his eye. "Do you not agree?"

"Yes!" she answered quickly, very nearly swooning with relief. "I think it an excellent notion."

Honor exhaled noisily, as if she had been running a very long distance. Her fears had not been realized. In fact, she had been granted a reprieve, a breathing spell in which she would not be cornered into confessing her crime or defending her virtue. Nor would she be required to concoct more lies—with the exception of the quite preposterous tale that she and Edmond wished to keep the particulars of their wedding to themselves.

It was as if a weight had been removed from her shoulders, for Honor had discovered that one of the most unnerving and exhausting consequences of prevarication was that one was obliged to remember every detail of what one had invented.

Encouraged by this happy turn of events, she was emboldened to ask, "How long must I . . . what I mean to say is, how long will *we* remain at the Park?"

Edmond seemed not to notice her slip of the tongue. "A fortnight. Perhaps less. You need remain only as long as it takes to convince Lady Raleigh to remove elsewhere. From her letters, I cannot believe she wants for sense, and once she understands that you and I mean to make Raleigh Park our home, it is likely she will lose no time in making other arrangements for herself and her daughter."

"And after that?"

"I had thought," he said airily, "that once the ladies were gone, you might wish to return to your family for a short visit. I, of course, will remain at the Park, to . . . er . . . make it comfortable for your return."

It was as though Honor's prayers had been answered. She need not go immediately to London. Furthermore, she would be in a place where Jerome Wade would never think to look for her. A fortnight gave her plenty of time to write to Uncle Wesley, to apprise him of what had happened and await his reply. Perhaps he could go to the agency for her to see if there was another family in need of a governess; if so, she might travel directly to a new position.

She need only play a role for a while, and once her part was finished, Edmond would send her to whatever town she claimed as her home. Easy enough. Actually, it was a simple plan. So simple that for just one moment, the thought flitted across Honor's brain that this had all come about too easily; especially considering all the trouble she had encountered previously. Lost in that rather depressing reflection, she failed to hear what he was saying. "I beg your pardon, sir."

"I merely asked if we were agreed upon our stories."

When she nodded, Edmond leaned back against the yellow-trimmed black squabs of the coach, a look of immense satisfaction on his face. To Honor, the smile that lurked in his eyes seemed almost smug, as though he had accomplished a complicated maneuver and was now congratulating himself upon his acumen. However, she elected not to question his motives overlong. After all, her own actions would not withstand close scrutiny.

Cheered at the thought of leaving her troubles behind even for a short while, she removed her handkerchief from her reticule and wiped the frost from the berlin's window. Free now to enjoy the scenery, she gave herself up to the perusal of the Devon countryside, or as much of it as she could see, for at the moment they were on a narrow road, descending into a wooded valley.

Very soon they neared the picturesque little market town of Abbingdon, and thinking she might never pass this way again, Honor stared with interest. A small inn, a stone church complete with a tall steeple, eight or ten shops, and a cluster of thatched mud cottages—their great square chimneys plastered over and washed yellow—made up the town.

As the coach slowed to traverse the high street, then resumed speed, continuing westward, Honor observed the rather odd cottages of the area. *Untidy* she thought them at first. But as she grew accustomed to their washed cob walls and their haphazardly placed windows, she began to discern a certain charm in the carelessness that was quite pleasing.

"The area is beautiful in the spring," Edmond said, as though he read her thoughts. "With the orchards in bloom and the hedgerows dotted all about with pink and blue and yellow wildflowers, I cannot believe Abbingdon has an equal."

Surprised at his rather proprietary observation, Honor asked if he had been reared at Raleigh Park.

"I have been there twice only, but it is a very special place, a place one does not easily forget. My grandmother was born at Raleigh Park, and my father had run tame there when a lad. He was a great favorite with his uncle and his cousin, Frederick, and he wanted me to know them and the land. Though not on a grand scale, the Park was the closest thing to a family seat we could claim, for my father was a military man, and like so many military families, our homes were usually leased."

Honor detected a note of wistfulness in his voice, and though she understood about the nomadic life of the military family, she kept the information to herself.

For a time Edmond said no more, remaining silent as though lost in thoughts he did not wish to share. Then, as the coach passed a cottage quite close to the road and was forced to swerve to avoid a pair of chickens, he began to laugh. The fowl—one white, one a muddy brown—had jumped for their lives, landing on the low cob wall adjoining the dwelling, where they registered their protests with a series of loud and indignant squawks.

"A fitting welcome," he said, "and one I fear may be repeated when we reach Raleigh Park."

When Honor raised her eyebrows in question, he said, "Entails. They may serve their purpose of keeping profligate heirs from selling the land off a piece at a time, but one can hardly expect those family members who are dispossessed in favor of some unknown heir to appreciate the overall effectiveness of the system."

Honor was saved the necessity of a reply when the carriage turned in at a massive gray stone gateway. The wrought iron gates stood open, a circumstance that obviously prevailed, since the lodge appeared to be uninhabited. The carriageway was long and winding, with a stand of high elms off to the left, and three joined outbuildings—possibly greenhouses—to the right. Snow covered what Honor suspected might be a handsome expanse of lawn leading up to the front of the house.

As the coachman halted the horses before the low, rambling white building, Honor was immediately attracted by the handsome stone-mullioned windows. They seemed to her like the smiling eyes of a friend, welcoming, and bidding one enter and be refreshed.

"It is lovely," she said.

"Yes. Though the inside was far from fashionable the last time I saw it, it was always a comfortable house. Sir Frederick, my father's cousin, was a loud, cheerful fellow with a fondness for company, hence the open gates. Unfortunately, he also had a love of boisterous, seemingly untrainable dogs. The animals roamed the house at will, and as you can imagine, the smell of wet dog fairly permeated the rooms."

Honor wrinkled her nose in distaste, making Edmond chuckle, but his laughter turned into a sharply indrawn breath when the front door opened and a young woman in the first blush of youth stepped outside. She paused on the portico, her hand resting upon a graceful, Ionic column, a smile of welcome on her lips.

A slender, delicate blonde, she was dressed in the lilac of half mourning, with a Norwich shawl thrown around her shoulders to protect her from the cold, and she was easily the most beautiful creature Honor had ever seen.

While Honor stared, speechless, the valet jumped down from his place atop the coach and opened the door. Edmond lost no time in descending the carriage steps and approaching the young lady. "How do you do?" he said, making her an elegant bow. "I am Edmond Lawrence, Sir Frederick Raleigh's cousin."

The beauty looked up at him with eyes the vibrant green of holly leaves washed by a summer shower. "Cousin Edmond," she said, her voice soft and breathy. "You have come at last."

Edmond smiled with the aplomb of a practiced rogue. "*Cousin,* did you say? May I ask, fair vision, who it is I have the pleasure of addressing?"

The vision giggled entrancingly, though she placed her fingertips against her pretty lips as if to contain the youthful sound. "I pray you, Cousin, do not make sport of me. You must know who I am."

"Forgive me, happy maiden, but I do not."

The giggles abated, replaced by a look of bewilderment. "But I am Dinah Moseby, cousin. Your betrothed."

Chapter 6

When the valet handed Honor down from the carriage, and she heard the startling information that Edmond possessed a fiancé, she experienced a most unfamiliar longing to faint and be removed from the entire scene. Unfortunately, that outlet of escape was denied her.

If Edmond wished for a similar deliverance, she saw no sign of it, save, perhaps that slight twitch of muscle in his left jaw.

"Honor, my dear," he said, taking her unwilling hand and drawing it within the crook of his arm, as if he had done so a million times before, "allow me to present my new and very lovely cousin, Miss Dinah Moseby." He found it necessary to adjust the snugness of his cravat before adding, "Cousin Dinah, I make you known to Mrs. Lawrence."

Breathing deeply to fortify herself, Honor waited for an outcry of some kind from Edmond's betrothed. Strangely, nothing happened. The chit merely executed a graceful curtsy, then invited them into the house, all the time smiling and chatting happily about how glad her mother would be to see them.

It was only when they joined Lady Raleigh in the red

drawing room that the reason for the girl's sangfroid became evident.

"Mother," Dinah said, "here is our cousin come to us at last, and he has brought us a pleasant surprise. His sister is with him. Edmond, Miss Lawrence, this is my mother."

Rowina Raleigh came forward, her hand outstretched and a smile of welcome upon her pretty face. There was about her the soft scent of flowers, and the aroma floated gently upon the air as she moved. A widow of seven months, the collar and sleeves of her green faille dress bore the black trim of mourning.

Looking at the woman, who was on the sunny side of forty, Honor could easily believe that she had once been every bit as breathtaking as Dinah. Still most attractive, she possessed the same blond hair, the same green eyes, the same delicate bone structure of her daughter, and a stranger might be forgiven for thinking the two of them sisters.

"Cousin Edmond," Lady Raleigh said as he lifted her knuckles to his lips, "how happy I am to welcome you to your new home." With a smile every bit as warm as the one she had bestowed upon the new heir, she turned to Honor. "Miss Lawrence, it is a pleasure to make your acquaintance. Though, to tell the truth, I had thought Cousin Edmond an only child."

"Lady Raleigh, I . . ." Like a coward, Honor turned to Edmond.

That muscle in his jaw no longer twitched—it positively leapt. "I fear there had been a misunderstanding, ma'am. Honor is not *Miss* Lawrence. She is my wife."

The hush that followed this announcement was dispelled by a gasp from Dinah. Reluctantly, Honor turned to face the startled young lady, who blinked back the tears glistening in her eyes.

"No," Dinah said. "It cannot be true. You are roasting me, sir." The tears would be contained no longer; they spilled over, coursing down her silken cheeks. "I might have known you would be like Papa Frederick, for he delighted in teasing me. Times out of mind he would—"

"Dinah!" Lady Raleigh interrupted. "Say no more, please."

The girl looked from her mother's ashen face to Edmond's purposefully bland countenance before turning and fleeing the room, slamming the door behind her.

Though it was obvious to Honor that Rowina Raleigh wanted to follow her daughter, the lady made a visible effort to control her emotions, forcing a smile to her trembling lips. "Cousin Honor," she said quietly, "I offer you my felicitations and wish you much happiness in your marriage and your new home."

Honor mumbled some sort of reply. What it was, she could not even guess, but it was definitely not the words that were running through her brain, for those words accused her of being the most despicable creature in nature.

Somehow she found herself seated beside Edmond on one of two red damask sofas that faced each other across a low, black lacquer table. Decorated in the Chinese motif of the Prince Regent's Brighton Pavilion, the recently renovated drawing room gave onto the expansive front lawns by way of double French windows. At the bottom of the room, mahogany pocket doors stood open, revealing portions of a handsome library.

A large, welcoming fire blazed beneath a black marble mantel, which was topped by an intricately carved pediment picked out in gold leaf. Unfortunately, the fire offered little comfort to one who knew herself to have destroyed a young girl's future.

This entire misunderstanding was her fault, and as Honor sipped from the pale cream and green Worcester teacup, she prayed the steaming Bohea would dissolve the lump that seemed permanently stuck in her throat.

She contributed little more than monosyllables to the conversation, focusing her attention upon the red, black, and gold patterned Axminster carpet, as though the plush yarn might tell her how she was to reveal the truth about her counterfeit marriage without putting herself in jeopardy once again.

While Honor pondered the web of lies that would not cease tangling, Edmond contemplated his own part in the young girl's disappointment. Though he did not believe for an instant that the chit's heart was engaged, or that she would suffer overlong, telling the lie had been more difficult that he had imagined.

His own discomfort notwithstanding, the incident demonstrated to a nicety the wisdom of bringing a wife to Raleigh Park. If he had come alone, the conversation of the moment might possibly have consisted of marriage settlements and jointures; instead, it was made up of nothing more consequential than Lady Raleigh's passion for the exotic flowers in the greenhouses.

As an officer and a gentleman, Edmond was accustomed to playing the pretty while enduring dull military socials, and that training allowed him to smile and respond suitably to Lady Raleigh's comments, making such remarks as the occasion demanded. All the while, he reflected upon his near escape, thanking those powers of heaven and earth responsible for turning over his post chaise and not allowing him to continue to Abbingdon alone.

All he need do, he told himself, was keep up the pretense until Dinah and Lady Raleigh quit the Park. To strengthen his charade, it behooved him to bestow upon Honor all those little attentions newly married men were want to show their brides. To that end, he made a mental note to be particularly careful to touch her upon occasion and to invite her for quiet walks in the shrubbery.

Thinking it as good a time as any to begin the game, he set his cup and saucer on the small ebony table at his elbow and reached across the red seat cushion that separated him from Honor; his plan, to give her rather tightly clenched fist a husbandly squeeze. To Edmond's astonishment, when his fingers touched hers, her hand turned over and clasped his tightly, as though she were drowning and he were her lifeline.

Yet even more amazing than her action was his own reaction, for when their palms touched, a frisson of awareness shot through him—awareness as surprising as it was heated. Before he could assimilate that unforeseen repercussion, however, she twined her fingers with his, and he was dealt another surprise, an instant feeling of camaraderie. Almost as if they were in this together, the two of them against the world.

Pure foolishness, of course. Females had their place in the scheme of things, but only an addle-pate would believe it possible for a man and a woman to be comrades—to sustain one another in time of trouble.

Edmond knew for a fact that women were incapable of such friendship. There was something lacking in their character; their basic makeup included neither loyalty nor trustworthiness. He had only to look to his mother to know this was true. Had his mother not made a cuckold of his father, then married Lord Frome scarce six months after Carlton Lawrence's death? And for what? Friendship? Love? Hardly. Like all women, she married him for one thing, and one thing only, for wealth and social position.

Unthinkingly, Edmond must have put undue pressure on Honor's fingers, for she stiffened and tried to pull away. Though he relaxed his hold, he did not let her go; instead, he made a show of raising her hand to his lips. Just before bending his head to brush a kiss against her skin, he smiled and said, "Your pardon, my love."

Edmond had meant the gesture purely for Lady Raleigh's edification. Nevertheless, when he lifted his head again, and his gaze locked with Honor's, it was he who learned the lesson. He encountered a look of such distress in her eyes that he was obliged to stop himself from taking her in his arms and assuring her that all would be well.

Before he could act upon this instinct, however, Honor snatched her hand away. As well, she put an end to any thoughts he might have entertained of recapturing that moment of camaraderie by rising from the sofa and asking if she might be shown to her room.

"Of course," Lady Raleigh replied, standing almost as quickly as Honor. "Traverchick?" she said, motioning to the elderly butler who stood near the door, ready to fetch teacups or pass around the plate of cakes should the need arise. "The room? Is it . . ."

"All is in readiness, m'lady."

After bowing to Lady Raleigh, then to Honor, the stoop-shouldered, gray-haired servant opened the door, beckoning to a maid who must have been waiting just outside in the vestibule. Instantly, she stepped forward and bobbed a curtsy.

"Cousin Honor," Lady Raleigh said, "Celia will show you to your room. If you have need of a rest after your journey, there is ample time for a nap before dinner. It is our custom to keep country hours here, but I am certain Cook could hold dinner until six or six-thirty if necessary."

"No. Please. I do not wish to be a bother."

"How could anything you desire be a bother? Raleigh Park is your home now, and you are the new chatelaine." Lady Raleigh paused, a slight unsteadiness in her voice. "At your convenience, I am prepared to turn over the keys."

Her face warm with embarrassment, Honor was on the verge of denying any desire to possess the keys, when she recollected that Edmond expected her to help him ease the present occupants of the house from the premises. Though it was the way of the world for widows to step aside in favor of the new heir's wife, it seemed a harsh way, and after having met the ladies, Honor was not certain she could do as Edmond asked. Especially not now, when she knew that one of those to be ousted was his fiancé.

Had Edmond forgotten that important piece of information when he spoke of their removal? His memory had seemed quite lucid when he described the house. Yet he had spoken of the ladies almost as though he had never met them, referring to them simply as his cousin's widow and her daughter.

Could that casual reference have been for Honor's benefit? Since he believed himself married to her, had he not mentioned Dinah to spare Honor pain? For all she knew, Edmond was putting a good face on the situation in deference to her, all the time aching inside for having abandoned his betrothed. The idea left Honor feeling lower than a London louse.

She could not let her lies destroy the lives of three innocent people. She must do something. But first she must have some answers from Edmond.

Mumbling something to Lady Raleigh about leaving the matter of the keys for another day, Honor hurried out to the vestibule where a diminutive young maid in a crisply starched mobcap and apron waited, ready to lead her up the broad, curving staircase.

As she followed the servant, who could not have been more than fourteen years of age, Honor wondered how she was to find a moment alone with Edmond to ask him about Dinah. To her chagrin, she soon discovered that she had been shown to the master suite, and that speaking to the new owner of the house involved nothing more complicated than passing through a dressing room connecting his bedchamber with her own.

Not that she meant to do so! Not ever.

"That be the way to the master's room," Celia had informed her, her still childish voice hushed with awe. "Mr. Crispin be in there now setting out the master's things."

Not wanting to expose herself as the fraud she was—not if she could find another way—Honor tried to act in a manner befitting a legitimate wife only just arrived in her new home. Feigning an interest in the predominantly blue bedchamber, she looked about her at the tasteful furnishings. "Very pretty," she said.

"The room be beautiful," Celia said, her pale gray eyes dreamy with admiration.

When Honor ran an idle finger along the blue-and-silver striped hangings on the half tester bed, she caught a whiff of flowers—the same subtle scent that clung to Rowina Raleigh—and with something very like a blow to the midsection, she realized the apartment had been the private domain of Lady Raleigh. Probably as recently as an hour ago.

Before the lady ordered the tea, then sat in the drawing room, pouring bohea and making small talk with the interlopers as though her life had not just been tossed over the moon, she must have instructed someone to come up and remove her personal items, then place them in a smaller, less significant chamber.

As if confirming Honor's suspicion about the room's previous occupant, the maid said, "Sir Frederick had everything done fresh before him and her ladyship pledged their troths."

Cautiously, Celia ran her work-roughened hands across the back of a blue velvet fauteuil—one of a pair of upholstered armchairs positioned comfortably close to the flames that danced orange and yellow beneath the white marble mantel. Honor chose not to sit in one of the chairs presumably intended for cozy *tête-à-tête* between husband and wife, but walked over to a little fruitwood dressing table with a hanging looking glass. Just in front of the table was a stool covered in the same blue and silver as the bed hangings, and for want of anything better to do, she sat there and listened to the maid chatter on about her previous employer.

"Weren't nothing too good for the new bride. Aunt Clara—she be the cook here—said as how it were because of Sir Frederick being so much older. Nearly old enough to be her ladyship's father, and fair taken with her from the day he clapped eyes on her. Wanted to give her the world; her and Miss Dinah both. Even turned his dogs out of the house, he did. And that was a thing nobody ever expected to see."

She *tsk-tsked*. "Too bad he were took so soon. Scarce

back from their wedding trip, they were, when the influenza felled him. T'were a real shame."

The girl ducked her head, as if recalling that Sir Frederick's demise was the reason why Edmond Lawrence was new master of Raleigh Park.

Wanting to let the child know she was not offended, Honor said, "How long have you worked here?"

"Nigh on a year, ma'am. There were another mouth to feed at home—that be eight in all—so Aunt Clara got me the job here."

"Your family must be proud of you."

With a matter-of-fact shrug she replied, "Leastways, they be right proud of the quid I send home each Quarter Day."

She stretched to her full, if insignificant, height, her little round face taking on a determined look. "But I don't plan to scrub floors and lay fires forever. I got ambitions, I have. Someday I mean to be a dresser for a great lady." She paused, as if enjoying the image conjured up by the statement. "Mayhap I'll get so famous all the other great ladies will try to steal me away to work for them, slipping gelt in my apron pocket just so I'll consider their offers, on account of me being so good at my job."

A smile threatened Honor's lips, but she forced them to behave. "And are you that good, Celia?"

"Yes'um. That's how come Mr. Traverchick give me this chance to look after you until your own maid arrives. I got a real way with hair, and once I sew a seam, it don't never come undone. And when I set a stitch, it be so tiny a body needs a quizzing glass just to find it. Her ladyship's woman be forever asking me to show her how I fashion my little floss rosebuds, but I keep my secrets, I do."

The child seemed to realize she was talking too much and bobbed a curtsy. "I'll take good care of your things, ma'am. You don't need to worry about me breaking nothing, nor scorching your linens. Only . . ." For a moment she fell silent, her face suffusing with color. "Begging your pardon, I'm sure, ma'am, but didn't nobody bring up ought be a small valise. Be your trunks coming by wagon?"

"My trunk seems to have gone astray," Honor said, glad the reply was at least a half truth.

The maid's mouth fell open. "You mean you've nothing but the things in the valise?"

"And this," she replied, lifting a fold of the maroon kerseymere, then letting it fall back against her lap. "I am sorry to disappoint you, Celia, but your journey toward becoming a great lady's dresser will not begin with me."

Though the incredulity on the child's face was almost comical, Honor was not tempted to laugh, finding the prospect of surviving a fortnight with only one dress to her name far from amusing. Not wishing to contemplate the situation, she gave her attention to her meager assortment of toiletries, which had been laid out upon the polished top of the little table. She had just picked up her brush when there was a knock at the dressing room door.

"May I come in?" Edmond asked.

"Please do," she responded. No point in standing on formality now, not after they had spent two nights in the same inn room. And especially not when she needed to talk with him. She put down the brush and turned to watch him as he strolled into the room, totally at his ease in a lady's bedchamber.

Apparently, the loquacious Celia was struck speechless by the sight of her new master, resplendent in skin-tight fawn pantaloons, highly polished Hessians, a buff twill waistcoat, and a morning coat of Cambridge blue that was a subtle compliment to his medium brown hair and eyes. Tall, broad-shouldered, and well-muscled, he must have appeared a veritable giant to the diminutive maid, for she could do nothing but stare, her jaw slack and her eyes round as saucers.

Apparently accustomed to strong reactions, Edmond said, "If your work is done, you may go."

"Y . . . yes, sir."

Though he had spoken kindly, the moonstruck girl bobbed a quick curtsy and rushed from the room as if pursued by Beelzebub himself—in her haste, leaving the door ajar.

Exasperated, Edmond walked over to perform the office, muttering something beneath his breath about being gaped at like an attraction in a raree show. Listening to him, Honor smiled for the first time since leaving the carriage. The reaction was not to her credit, but after having been judged wanting by so many people these past few days, it made her feel better somehow to see the mighty Edmond Lawrence put out of countenance by a strangers' response to him.

Choosing to ignore Honor's smile, he glanced around the room. "A very handsome apartment. I suppose I have Lady Raleigh to thank for this show of taste."

"And have you noticed?" Honor asked, sniffing meaningfully, "no wet dog smell."

This time Edmond smiled. "For that, you may believe me exceedingly grateful."

"I collect, sir, that you are not a dog lover."

"And I collect, madam, that you wish to trap me into an unflattering admission. Therefore, even if I detested dogs, which I do not, I should not admit to the fact, lest you gawk at me gape-mouthed, like that child in the mobcap."

"Acquit me, sir, for I try never to gawk. I should more likely scowl at you and think to myself that there was something lacking in your character."

Edmond's mouth twitched, but he managed to maintain a sober countenance. "Actually, I am quite fond of the beasts. But one or two at a time."

"And preferably with a long pedigree?"

He shook his head. "I assure you, I am not so high in the instep as all that. As a matter of fact, I was once sincerely attached to a floppy-eared hound of dubious ancestry given to me by my father on the occasion of my fifth birthday. Father judged the mutt to be of primarily German origin, so I named him George, in honor of the king."

Honor laughed. "Never say so."

"Ah, but I already have. Remember, I was only five."

"I suppose it was an innocent enough tribute from a boy of tender years. But I do hope the king was never apprised of this questionable show of respect."

Edmond chuckled, and after asking her permission, seated himself in one of the velvet chairs. "My father did not travel in the king's set, so there was no fear of His Majesty learning of his new namesake. However, I must inform you that nature soon showed me the error of my ways."

"How was that, sir?"

"Within the year, George dropped a litter of pups. A thoroughly misbegotten lot. Eleven in all."

"E . . . eleven?" Honor could not contain her laughter. "Poor George."

"Be that as it may, once I saw the litter, I agreed to

abandon the original appellation for something more fitting."

"A wise decision, sir. One can only hope you chose a name not quite so disrespectful."

"On the contrary. Since the mutt had produced such a bumper crop of unhandsome offspring, my father suggested I call her Charlotte, after the queen."

Honor gasped, then went into whoops. "He never!"

"I assure you, he did."

Wiping the tears of laughter from her eyes, Honor said, "I think I like your father."

The words were spoken spontaneously, and as Edmond watched her dab unself-consciously at the tears, using the cuff of her dress sleeve, he had a rather disturbing suspicion that his father would have liked her as well.

Though she was not the type of female his mother would consider a social equal, Edmond felt quite certain that Carlton Lawrence would have appreciated Honor's quiet, good manners and the way she made the best of a situation. Like a well-bred filly faced with a new jump, she showed courage. His father would have said she had *heart*.

Looking at the woman whose background and motives were mysteries he had yet to solve, Edmond decided his father would have been right; whoever, and whatever she was, she definitely had heart. And, lest he forget it, compassion. Had she not taken care of him when he was ill?

He continued to study her, and as she became aware of his appraisal, the laughter died on her lips, and a hint of color touched her creamy complexion. Their eyes met, softly holding for an instant, and Edmond could almost believe he felt the warmth of her skin, as if she were sitting in the chair next to his instead of perched on a stool halfway across the room. And for one unbelievably crazy moment, he was obliged to fight the desire to go to her and catch her face within his hands, to feel the warmth, the texture, for real.

Whoa, old man. Dangerous! That way lies all manner of hidden traps.

It behooved Edmond to remember the purpose for which he had come to her chamber. It was to see if he could discover why she had appeared so distressed just before she left the drawing room. It was definitely *not* to be distracted by the texture of her skin.

"May I ask you something?" he said rather quickly.

Honor very nearly replied in the affirmative, so mesmerized was she by that look he had given her. She had felt his gaze touching her, and the sensation had sent a warmth coursing through her, almost as if he had touched her with his hands.

No, no. He must not touch me. Nor must I wish him to touch me.

She reminded herself that she was prohibited from even entertaining such thoughts, for Edmond was betrothed to Dinah. Furthermore, Honor had vowed to see if she could discover his true feelings about the young lady, and to reunite the pair if possible.

"No," she said, in answer to his question, "you may ask me nothing." She straightened her spine as if that would strengthen her resolve. "Have you forgotten, sir? It was your edict that you should regain your memory without any assistance from me."

"Yes. But—"

"We agreed to the plan, and I shall not renege."

Edmond ran his fingers through his hair, mussing it so that several strands fell across his forehead, making him appear more relaxed, almost vulnerable, and Honor found it necessary to harden her heart against the effect this small act had upon her resolve. "I—"

"Ma'am?" Celia called, scratching upon the door.

"Come in," Honor replied, happy to have this meeting with Edmond interrupted, even though it meant she would not be allowed to ask her own question, to learn if he truly loved Dinah.

Opening the chamber door a fraction, the maid poked her head around the edge. The rest of her remained on the other side as she observed her new master, apparently ready to swoon if he so much as glanced in her direction.

To her surprise, Honor no longer found the girl's adolescent admiration of Edmond amusing, and she spoke more sharply than she had intended. "Come in, Celia, for heaven's sake. Mr. Lawrence will not bite you."

Suddenly remembering that he had said almost those same words to her in the coach, she looked at him to see if he recalled the incident. From the light in his eyes, he did, and the fact that he remembered produced a flush of pleasure that warmed Honor clear to her toes.

Warning herself that she must not participate in such intimacies as sharing private jokes, she returned her attention to the maid. "What do you want?"

"Begging your pardon, ma'am, but I came to show you this." She stepped just inside the room. Folded across her arm was a rose sarcenet dress. "Lady Raleigh's abigail gave it to me to see if you would consider wearing it to dinner. It be Miss Dinah's, but her ladyship said she would be pleased to see it disappear forever from Miss Dinah's clothespress. On account of her having yellow hair, don't you know, and rose being a color meant for ladies with dark hair."

Edmond stared at the dress, then jerked his thumb toward the door, signaling for the maid to leave them. As soon as she was gone, he turned his attention to Honor. The relaxed, approachable man of a moment ago was gone, and in his place stood a man with anger in his aspect, almost as if he had been offered an insult and meant to challenge the miscreant to a duel.

"This question I will ask you, ma'am. And I expect an answer. Why should anyone so forget herself as to offer my wife another woman's castoffs?"

Honor considered refusing to answer, on the basis of her not actually being his wife, but the anger in Edmond's eyes convinced her that the prize of victory would not be worth the cost of the battle. Furthermore, in this instance, she felt certain she would lose.

"My trunk is on its way to London, and I have nothing save the clothes I am wearing."

As if only just now noticing, he looked at the maroon kerseymere. A good color for her, but he misliked the style; it made her resemble a governess. "And why is your trunk bound for London?"

"Because my home is in London, and *I* was bound there when we met."

Chapter 7

Honor stepped from the luxury of a hot tub, and though she would not allow Celia to towel her back or help her don her freshly laundered drawers and shift, she was perfectly agreeable to sitting before the dressing table to let the maid brush out her hair.

"Cooee," she said after Honor released the pin from the twisted knot atop her head and let the thick hair fall about her shoulders. "Such lovely hair, ma'am. Fair reminds me of the sky on a moonless winter night. Not quite black, but near enough as makes no never mind."

"Why, Celia, do you aspire to become a poet as well as a famous dresser?"

A giggle her only reply, the maid began to brush out the long tresses, assessing the hair texture with each stroke, deciding how best to arrange it. She had just begun a few experimental twists and pulls when there was a knock at the outer door.

"Mrs. Lawrence?" came the inquiry. The voice was Dinah's.

When Celia opened the door, the young lady stepped inside the room, her beautiful face flushed with embarrassment, her green eyes downcast. "Forgive me for intruding, Mrs. Lawrence, but I have come to apologize.

I . . ." She looked up, and once again her eyes were filled with tears. "I behaved badly. And . . . and I had no right to—"

"You had every right to be surprised," Honor said, obeying an instinct and walking over to the girl. Taking both her hands, she guided her to the chairs before the fireplace. Dinah went willingly and disposed herself opposite Honor, arranging the skirt of her jonquil muslin with care so it did not become crushed. The tears had all but vanished.

"Mother is cross as crabs with me and predicts I shall soon find myself performing on the stage if I do not guard against what she calls a predisposition toward histrionics."

"No, no, my dear. You were dealt a severe shock." Honor reached across the space that separated them and patted the young lady's hand. "In your place, anyone must have felt it."

Dinah blinked, as if much struck by this championing of her behavior. "Well, that is just what I thought, only mother said—" She stopped herself. "I shall not get into that now, or I shall forget my reason for intruding upon you when you are busy dressing for dinner."

"You could never intrude."

The girl smiled prettily. "Then you accept my apology?"

"I will if it pleases you, but there is something I would say to you first."

Dinah leaned forward, interest writ clearly upon her face, but as she did so, Honor recalled that they were not alone. Celia stood over by the dressing table, pretending not to hear what was being said, and though Dinah had been reared in the company of servants, and obviously could ignore their presence, Honor could not. "What I have to say can wait. And as you say, I should be getting dressed."

The girl rose politely. "Tomorrow, then?"

Honor nodded. "Yes. Tomorrow we will talk."

"I shall look forward to it, for you cannot know how I have longed to have someone with whom to enjoy a comfortable coze. I adored dear Papa Frederick, and I would not have wanted to be any place but here with him and Mama, but it has been lonely without the friends I knew in Kent."

"You have made no new friends here?"

"There has been no opportunity, for we have been in mourning almost from the time of our arrival."

The information made Honor's heart feel as though someone had tied it to a large stone and tossed it into an abyss. Poor, dear Dinah. The girl had been separated from her home and friends, and now she believed herself to have been jilted.

"Begging your pardon, ma'am," Celia said, interrupting Honor's thoughts, "but the gong be sounding any minute now. I need time to help you into your dress and to do up your hair."

Dinah had arrived at the door, but she paused, her hand on the knob, a smile upon her face. "Until later, Cousin."

"Please. If we are to be friends, you must call me Honor."

With a smile sparkling enough to challenge the most costly diamond, Dinah waved a farewell and left the room.

The instant the door closed, Honor hurried over to the dressing table where Celia stood, ready to help her step into the sarcenet frock.

Easing the dress upward, she said, "It should fit well

enough for now, ma'am, you and Miss Dinah both being slender, but if we find it needs letting out a little in the bosom, I can see to that tomorrow." The maid pulled the tiny sleeves up over Honor's shoulders, then began doing up the tapes in the back. "I tarried too long removing all them bows and rosettes as had been tacked around the neckline, and had only just finished letting the hem down so your ankles wouldn't show, when the bath arrived. But," she said, giving the sleeves a final straightening, "I think you'll like the result."

Pausing in her chattering, Celia gazed at Honor in the looking glass. Despite the maid's earlier bravado, her face was filled with apprehension. "You do like it, don't you, ma'am?"

Honor was certain she had never seen a more elegant dress. Without a doubt, she had never worn anything quite so lovely. A dusty rose that leant a sheen to her dark hair, the twilled silk was cut along simple lines, with a high waist and a gently tapered skirt. Every embellishment had been removed from the garment, save a delicately embroidered rose placed just in the left corner of the square neckline. Celia's instincts had been right on the button; there was no need for decorations—far better to let the beauty of the material work its own magic.

Smiling at the maid, Honor said, "You are truly a magician, and I prophesy a long and prosperous career for you."

As mistress and maid admired the result, the dinner gong sounded, breaking in upon their respective thoughts.

Celia recovered first. "Your hair, ma'am! Sit down and let me see what I can do with it."

"No, no." Suddenly nervous that she might appear a

figure of fun to her dinner companions if she sported a new hair style *and* borrowed finery, Honor said she would do her own hair. "For I have no wish to be late, and I still need shoes and stockings."

Ignoring the maid's disappointment, Honor bent forward and twisted the long strands as she had done every day since she first put her hair up nine years ago. While she pinned the knot on top of her head, then fluffed out a few wispy curls along her forehead and in front of her ears, Celia knelt on the floor and slipped the white silk stockings up over Honor's knees and tied the garters.

To the frustration of both females, the matching pink slippers did not fit. No matter how Celia pushed or pulled, Honor could not squeeze her entire foot into a slipper made for someone of Dinah's more delicate bone structure. Finally, practically in tears, the maid admitted defeat and fetched Honor's own half boots.

Seeing the sturdy leather toes protruding from beneath the silk hem, Celia's lip began to tremble. "Mayhap if you bent your knees a bit, ma'am."

Obediently, Honor bent until the dress touched the floor, momentarily hiding the substantial footwear. Not certain she could maintain such a pose, however, she straightened and patted the girl's shoulder.

"Never mind," Honor said, as much to cheer herself as the girl, "you did everything possible to turn me into the fairy-tale princess who went to the ball. The fault is not yours that I possess the feet of one of the wicked stepsisters."

Not at all amused by the little joke, Celia bristled, her face taking on the look of a bulldog ready to defend its prize bone. "Begging your pardon, ma'am, but you still look a picture." Fetching up the Norwich shawl she had borrowed from Lady Raleigh, she placed it around

Honor's shoulders, then took one last look at her handiwork. "You mark my words, Mr. Lawrence won't be able to take his eyes off you."

At the thought, Honor's face turned a shade to rival the dress. Whether the color in her cheeks was due to a hope that Edmond would *not* notice, or to a hope that he *would*, was a question whose answer she did not wish to ponder. However, it was a moot point, for at the moment she was late, and no matter what her reception, she must delay her departure no longer.

Hurrying from the bedchamber, she descended the stairs with all due speed, but just as her foot touched the last step, the knocker sounded at the front door. She paused. Because she was visible from the doorway, Honor was uncertain if she should make a speedy retreat across the vestibule to the drawing room, or stay where she was. Deciding that flight would make her appear gauche, she chose to remain at the bottom of the stairs, and while the aged butler answered the summons, she bent her knees slightly to ensure that her hem covered the toes of her boots.

"Yes, sir?" Traverchick said.

"Is this Raleigh Park?" asked a handsome blond gentleman of slender build and teasing gray eyes.

"It is, sir."

Removing his curly brim beaver as if confident of receiving a welcome, the caller said, "Splendid. I have come in search of my friend, Mr. Edmond Lawrence. Is he here?"

"I am sure I cannot say, sir."

The butler did not loosen his hold upon the door, nor did he invite the visitor to step inside, and the formality of his tone informed the gentleman just what he thought of persons who called, uninvited, at the dinner hour.

The gentleman merely chuckled at the frosty reception. "If you mean to snub me, my good man, you will be obliged to do better than that, for I will have you know I have been refused admittance by some of the most top-loftly butlers in London."

Not immune to such teasing from a personable young gentleman, Traverchick unbent enough to say he would see if Mr. Lawrence was at home.

"That's the ticket. Knew you were a right 'un."

"Whom shall I say is calling."

"Tell him Sidney Avery has come to see for himself if his old friend is still among the living."

Honor recognized the name immediately, having heard Edmond call it out many times in his troubled dreams. "Mr. Avery," she said, moving forward, her hand extended in greeting. "How kind of you to call."

Sidestepping the butler, the visitor entered the vestibule, smiling cheerfully and making Honor a very gallant bow. "Not at all, ma'am. It is you who are kind to acknowledge the acquaintance. I shall be ever in your debt."

After taking her hand and lifting it almost to his lips, he treated her to a smile that was guaranteed to win over the heart of any lady, be she friend or stranger. "I had no notion how, or even if, I would be received, but I bless you for not turning me away. Devilish cold out there, don't you know."

Never one to hold a grudge, Mr. Avery handed over his hat, coat, and gloves to the butler, completing the divestment with a cheeky remark that brought a reluctant smile to Traverchick's wrinkled face. "I told you it was useless to snub me, my good man. Someone always lets me in."

Turning once again to Honor, he said, "Since it is my

intention to pledge my undying allegiance and devotion to you, fair lady, may I know your name?"

Unable to stop the smile that pulled at her lips, she was about to inform him that she was Miss Honor Danforth, when the door to the drawing room was flung open, revealing Edmond standing in the doorway.

"Avery!" he said, staring in disbelief at the gentleman whose entire attention was focused on Honor. "I thought I heard your voice, but I could not credit my ears. What the devil are you doing here? Other than making a pest of yourself with the first lady you meet?"

"Edmond, Edmond," he remarked with a melodramatic shake of his head, "I see you are still consumed with jealousy at my success with the fair sex."

While the two friends pumped each other's hands, Mr. Avery said, "As to what I am doing here, allow me to inform you, old boy, that before you burst upon the scene, interrupting me in that deplorably rude manner, I was about to declare my eternal devotion to this lovely lady. And *she* was about to tell me her name."

"Mind your manners," Edmond said quietly, the serious tone of his voice contrasting with his friend's teasing manner. After a quick glance at the listening butler, Edmond put his hand beneath Honor's elbow and drew her next to him. "Otherwise, I shall refuse to present you to my wife."

Mr. Avery's fine-tuned social graces stopped him just short of an outright refutation of the claim, though his eyebrows lifted in patent disbelief. Observing the reaction, Edmond clamped his large hand upon the shoulder of the shorter, more slender man, very nearly causing the visitor to wince. "Whatever your thoughts, Avery, save them for later. All of them."

Seeing that his message was received, Edmond relaxed his hold. "At the moment, Lady Raleigh and her daughter are waiting in the drawing room, and unless I miss my guess, they shall soon be wishing all three of us back to London for being so thoughtless as to delay dinner."

Quick to recognize the widow's name, Mr. Avery winked at his friend, then asked if someone would see to his carriage. "Of course, I can easily return to the village if my arrival is inconvenient. But to own the truth, I am famished."

"When were you not?" Edmond remarked dryly. "But never mind. I feel certain we can trust Traverchick to see that the horses are attended, and that a room is prepared for you."

The butler bowed respectfully. "As you wish, sir."

"And now," Edmond said, opening the drawing room door for Honor, "let us join Lady Raleigh and Miss Moseby."

If Rowina Raleigh was put out of countenance by the arrival of a gentleman she had never seen before, she was too well bred to betray the fact. As for her daughter, that young miss was struck speechless by the appearance of the newcomer, displaying a shyness and decorum hitherto unsuspected by Edmond Lawrence.

For his friend's part, it was obvious that Avery was completely bowled over by the ethereal beauty of Miss Dinah Moseby. It was a situation Edmond looked upon with satisfaction, for he hoped the chit's interest in another gentleman might lessen the string of his own arrival with a wife in tow. Also, once the ladies saw there were other fish in the sea, the knowledge might facilitate their early withdrawal from Raleigh Park. Edmond was nothing if not resourceful—a trait he had developed in his Peninsular days, when there were too few supplies and too many battles—and he meant to make full use of his friend's unexpected visit.

While Edmond poured the newcomer a glass of sherry, Honor watched Mr. Avery, who, from all she could tell, was well and truly captivated by Dinah. Feeling as though a stake had just been driven through her heart at this new complication, Honor wondered how she was to handle the situation.

Naturally, the gentleman could not be faulted for his reaction to Dinah's beauty, nor for assuming the young lady was free to entertain his admiration. After all, he had no way of knowing that she was his best friend's fiancé. Nor was Honor at leisure to inform him of the fact. And with her hands tied, how was she to keep the handsome visitor from ruining her plans for bringing about a reconciliation between the betrothed pair?

Obviously, she could do nothing now, so she contented herself with sitting on the edge of the red brocade sofa, keeping her booted feet well covered by her skirt, and seeing what she could do to deflect Mr. Avery's attention from Dinah. "I collect, sir, that you and Edmond served together in the Peninsular."

Ignoring the startled look in Edmond's eyes that she was privy to this piece of information, she gave the newcomer her full attention, listening to the rather amusing tale he put forth, *the complete and unabridged truth*, or so he said, regarding the number of times he had personally saved Edmond's life. "And I refer not only to the war years," he said, "but to the entire five and twenty years of our acquaintance."

While Edmond's savior apprised the delighted ladies of two or three Herculean acts of heroism on his part, exploits that stopped just short of moving entire mountains single-handedly, Edmond studied Honor's smiling face, wondering, not for the first time, what capricious fate had thrown them together. It was obvious that she had the advantage of him where information was concerned, and he could only wonder that an adventuress had chosen not to use such a powerful weapon to her gain.

"Why, if we should both live to be octogenarians," Simon Avery said, reclaiming Edmond's attention, "it still would not allow the fellow time enough to repay the debt he owes me for repeatedly standing between him and calamity."

"No," Edmond replied, "but it would allow me time enough to put a bullet through your melodramatic hide. For, believe me, nothing short of a burial will purify the air after such patent prevarication."

When his feminine auditors dissolved into laughter, Simon Avery sighed dramatically. "It was ever thus, dear ladies. Gratitude is so fleeting."

"It is you who will be fleeting," Edmond advised, "if you do not cut line."

At this point the butler informed Lady Raleigh that dinner was served, whereupon Mr. Avery rose quickly and offered his right arm to Lady Raleigh and his left arm to Miss Dinah. "We blondes must stick together," he vowed. Then smiling, he added, "Or if that will not serve as excuse enough to allow me the pleasure of escorting two of the loveliest ladies I have ever beheld, give me but a moment, and I will think of another."

Rowina Raleigh laughed prettily and placed her hand upon his arm, and though her daughter placed her hand on his other arm, if she smiled, it was not apparent. Dinah kept her face looking downward, allowing a view of nothing but the top of her sun-kissed hair, its tresses drawn loosely back from the sides and secured at the back, one long, thick curl trailing along her elegant nape.

Though Honor was filled with foreboding at the ease with which both mother and daughter had been captivated by the newcomer, she detected on Edmond's face a look of satisfaction, as though he were pleased that his friend had so easily ingratiated himself with the ladies. She could only assume he had not noticed the way Mr. Avery was looking at Dinah, or the way Dinah was *not* looking at Mr. Avery.

"Shall we?" Edmond said, offering her his hand.

Placing her hand in his, she let him help her from the sofa. She expected him to lead her to the door immediately, but to her surprise he did not do so. Still holding her hand, he leaned his head down close to hers, speaking quietly, as though the words were for her ears only, and as the feathery softness of his breath touched her skin, a shiver of delight traveled the length of her spine.

"And how is it, ma'am, that you knew that Simon and I served together in the Peninsular?"

Not wanting him to see how disturbed she was by his nearness, she said, "Questions, sir? Again?"

Muttering something about being hoist by his own petard, Edmond pulled her hand through the crook of his arm, thereby capturing her arm and holding it close to his side. "I shall withdraw the question, but may I be allowed to comment upon your appearance?"

Not waiting for permission, he said, "You look lovely."

Unsure whether the breathlessness she experienced was a result of the unexpected gallantry, or because her arm was being held fast between his muscular forearm and his side, Honor replied quickly, "It is the dress that is lovely, sir. Magical is it not, what can be wrought by placing a few yards of silk in the hands of a talented seamstress?"

As if he had only just noticed the frock, Edmond looked her over from head to toe, pausing when he discovered the leather boots peeping from beneath the rose silk hem. Honor thought she felt his ribs move, and she stiffened, certain he was laughing at her, convinced he must be disgusted at such a lack of refinement. However, when he returned his gaze to her face, his countenance revealed neither condemnation nor laughter.

Mollified, Honor had almost regained her composure when he sent it racing off again by winking at her, as though they shared an amusing secret.

"There is magic here, indeed," he said. "But I beg to differ as to its source. I believe it has been wrought by the lady *wearing* the dress."

Chapter 8

Dinner was a spirited meal, and even before the turtle soup was removed with a braised veal and a dish of apricot fritters, Mr. Avery had them all laughing. As well as entertaining them with the latest *on dits* about Prinny and his aging *chère amie*, he shared with them a few interesting observations about Neville Hall, his family seat in East Sussex. Lady Raleigh had wisely chosen an informal seating, with the extra leaves removed from the large ebony table, so the five diners were within easy talking distance of one another.

"Typical countryside, don't you know," Mr. Avery said, beginning his catalogue of the features of East Sussex, "with never-ending hedgerows, stone walls, and fields dotted with sheep. And, of course, if one likes that sort of thing, there is the sea and the chalk cliffs."

From the sudden wistful tone of his voice, it was obvious to each of his listeners that he did, indeed, like that sort of thing. Almost as if he had not meant to disclose anything truly personal, he launched into a story about the gorse bushes near his home. "In all of England there are no gorse comparable to those near Neville Hall.

"*Vicious*," he said with a shudder, bringing smiles to the faces of his fellow diners. "Or so I thought when I was a lad. I was convinced that one particular bush was possessed, for each time I passed that way, it seemed to reach out and grab my leg, often leaving me scratched and bleeding, as though I had been set upon by thieves and robbers."

"Poor little boy," Dinah said, truly entering the conversation for the first time since the visitor had arrived, and forsaking the monosyllabic responses she had employed for the last hour.

Simon Avery rewarded this show of sympathy by concentrating upon the chit's face as though it were a work of art to be savored and appreciated. Only when he realized that he had abandoned his story and was staring did he end the awkward silence by asking Dinah what part of the country she called home.

"Kent," she answered without hesitation.

"You don't say so? I have a small estate in Kent. Not large, mind you, but a tidy, neatish sort of place. It was left to me by my maternal grandfather."

"Do you go there often, sir?"

"No. I spend most of my time in town, aside from Christmas and a few weeks in the summer when I return to Neville Hall to see my parents. I am the second son, don't you know, so my brother will be the next viscount and inherit the Hall. When that happens, I shall probably make the place in Kent my home."

"Kent is lovely," Dinah said. "Our home was near the little village of Klee, between Maidstone and Tunbridge Wells."

Mr. Avery was much struck by this information. "You don't say so? My place is scarce an afternoon's ride from Tunbridge Wells." He turned to Rowina Raleigh. "Do you still have the house there, Lady Raleigh?"

"I do, sir. The property was left to me by my first husband, Mr. Moseby, and though it passed into Sir Frederick's keeping upon our marriage, the lawyers for the estate have assured me that ownership of the house and lands have reverted to me."

Edmond should have been elated. Here was the information he wanted: Lady Raleigh had a home to return to, and it was in a place dear to the heart of her daughter. And yet, the thrill of having gained this intelligence was mitigated by the look he had seen cross Honor's face when Rowina Raleigh spoke of lawyers. The look was wary, almost as if Honor anticipated an attack by Avery's possessed gorse bush.

Now, of course, she concentrated on an almond tartlet, as though it were of great importance, her fork pushing the untasted sweet from one side of her plate to the other, and her head lowered so that Edmond could see nothing but the thick, lustrous, dark hair that was twisted and pinned atop her head.

What had lawyers to do with her? Whatever it was, Honor did not look like sharing the information. And *he* could not ask her any questions. Not for the first time since he had uttered that idiotic plan did he wish he could take it back. If something was bothering her, he wanted to know about it. But she would have to decide on her own to come to him. If she wanted help, she would have to ask for it.

Not that he cared, of course. Why should he? She was nothing to him; just a woman who had suddenly tumbled into his life and would walk away from it within a matter of days. She would go, and he would let her. In fact, he would be happy to see the last of her, just as he would be happy to see the last of Lady Raleigh and Dinah. Women were an entanglement he meant to avoid. Out for what they could get, the lot of them.

Even as he thought it, he pictured Honor as she had

looked a short while ago, standing beside him in the drawing room, her head held high, daring him to comment upon the scuffed walking boots that showed beneath her borrowed silk. Such an adorable mixture of pride and vulnerability. At that moment, if it had been within his power, he would have whisked her off to Madame Lisette's in London and purchased for her every pair of slippers on the premises. In fact, if it would have pleased her, he would have bought Honor everything in the shop.

Strangely, he knew the moment he thought it that buying out the shop would *not* have pleased her. Unlike the barques of frailty previously under his protection, Honor—the innocent adventuress—would have thrown the lot back in his face.

Suddenly realizing that everyone was looking at him as if expecting some kind of response, he excused himself for woolgathering, and asked whomever had spoken to him to repeat the statement.

"I inquired," Lady Raleigh said, "if you wished to be shown about the property tomorrow. You have only to say the word, and I will send a message over to Bert Lane, the bailiff, who has been eagerly awaiting your arrival."

"I should like that. Thank you. Are there any saddle horses in the stable? The berlin would hardly be appropriate for jaunting across the fields."

"No, Cousin, it would not; especially when one considers the heavy snows we have endured of late. Fortunately, there are several likely beasts in the stable. They are good stock, though none are as spirited as you might like for your personal mount, especially if you wish to ride to hounds."

"I shall not be hunting," Edmond said. "Though I do require an animal capable of bearing my weight."

"Of course you do, sir. With the exception of Bright Star

and Gallant Lady, both of whom belong to me, everything in the stable is part of the estate. I feel certain there must be one or two mounts that would do nicely for a gentleman of your size. You have but to choose the horse that pleases you. Or," she added, "there is Sir Frederick's Stanhope, as well as a dog cart. Both are in good condition."

Edmond shook his head. "A horse, I think."

The conversation became general once again, with Avery inquiring of Lady Raleigh if there was any likely fishing to be had in the neighborhood.

"I fear I have no knowledge, sir, regarding places for sport. Perhaps Traverchick or one of the stable lads can answer your questions." She seemed lost in memory for a moment, then collecting herself, she said, "Because my bereavement came so close upon the heels of my arrival in Devon, I have seen little of the countryside save a bit of the moors. Before his illness, Sir Frederick took me for a look at the famous wild ponies."

For the remainder of the pleasant dinner, conversation became centered upon Rowina Raleigh's hobby, which was growing exotic plants.

"I believe you told us," Edmond said, "that my cousin, Frederick, ordered the construction of several greenhouses for your use."

"Yes," she replied. "It was his wedding gift to me. Each of the three enclosures are heated, but the third one also includes an indoor irrigation system, for it is devoted to plants that grow upon other plants, deriving their nourishment from nothing save the air and water."

"You don't say so," Mr. Avery said, much struck by the idea of anything that grew without soil.

With the subject matter far from exhausted, Rowina Raleigh begged their pardon for boring on about her own interests. Then, after placing her napkin beside her plate, she rose from the table and led the two younger ladies from the room, leaving the gentlemen to their port.

The time-honored ritual notwithstanding, two circumstances prompted the old friends not to remain at table above a few minutes. The first was Edmond's vow never again to touch strong spirits, and the second was the impossibility of private talk, impossible because Traverchick felt it incumbent upon him to stay close at hand to top off Mr. Avery's glass after each sip. And once it became apparent that the old retainer was prepared to remain at his post until the entire store of port was exhausted, the gentlemen rose by mutual consent and made their escape.

When they entered the drawing room, they found only Dinah and Honor in residence, for Lady Raleigh had stolen a few moments to visit the greenhouses. A plant Sir Frederick had had shipped from South America was near its time to bloom, and because the delicate blossom appeared for only a few hours each year—and that during the moonlit hours—she was loath to risk missing the event.

Noting the absence of the young lady's mother, Mr. Avery went directly to Miss Moseby, who sat at an inlaid pianoforte whose square case was aligned with the wall. Pulling up a chair next to the girl, he watched spellbound as her talented fingers danced across the keys in a spirited little Mozartean piece.

Edmond joined Honor on one of the red sofas that flanked the fireplace. "Do you play?"

"Nowhere near as well as that," she replied, glancing across the room at the young girl whose jonquil-clad back swayed gently to the rhythm of her performance. "So if you have conceived the notion of asking me to replace Dinah at the instrument, I beg you to reconsider."

Edmond inclined his head in a mock bow. "Your display of modesty is duly noted. However, since it would seem that all young ladies dissemble when first asked to perform, I beg *you* to reconsider."

"Acquit me of such artifice, sir, for mine was no ploy for further entreaty. I meant merely to convey to you that I wished to spare us both embarrassment: I, because I will appear to disadvantage, and you, because you will be obliged to stick your fingers in your ears at the din."

Edmond chuckled. "A compelling argument, to be sure, but I am willing to take the risk. Would it persuade you to try your luck if I promised to sit beside you and turn the pages of the music for you?"

"No, sir. Not even if you promised to write the song."

Having delivered her decree, she underscored the finality of her decision by twisting around to reach a small leather-bound book that reposed on the table at her elbow. The movement lifted the hem of her skirt, exposing her boots and reminding Edmond of a subject he wished to pursue.

"I wondered," he said, watching her thumb through the missive, "if you would not like to avail yourself of Sir Frederick's gig tomorrow? Or is your handling of the ribbons on a par with your proficiency at the pianoforte?"

"Not on a par," she said. "Worse. For I have no skill whatsoever with the ribbons. But even if I possessed such a talent, why would I wish to borrow the gig?"

Realizing he was treading on sensitive ground, he said, "Promise not to fly into the boughs?"

Her blue eyes grew wide with distrust. "I have learned never to promise compliance prior to hearing the petition. One never knows down what steep path the simplest-sounding request may take one."

"Very wise. In this instance, however, I hope you may not find the path too precipitous. I merely thought you and

Dinah might drive into the village. Take a look in at the shops."

Honor lifted her delicately arched eyebrows, the gesture a fine blend of pride and hauteur. "And why should we wish to do that?"

Edmond flicked a minuscule speck of dust from the sleeve of his dark blue evening coat. This was proving more difficult than he had anticipated. A new experience for him, as he had never before felt the least reticence about offering a female a shopping trip; possibly because he had never before known a female who would refuse the offer.

"I thought Dinah might show you where you could purchase a few replacements for those items that are in the trunk that is on its way to London."

Color stole up Honor's neck to her face, prompting Edmond to wish he had chosen a more private place for this discussion. The wisdom of hindsight not withstanding, he continued. "Also, if there is a creditable modiste's, you might wish to—"

"No," she said, the word softly spoken, but none the less emphatic. "I assure you, such a trip is not necessary, for I—" The remainder of her words were rendered inaudible by Dinah's enthusiastic override.

"I should love it!" declared that maiden, her playing having ended just in time to overhear the suggestion. "Oh, Honor, if you only knew how I have missed going to the shops with a friend. What fun we shall have. Though you must understand, the shops are not at all what you will be accustomed to in London. Still, I shall find it such a treat."

"By Jove," Mr. Avery added, "we can make a day of it. If you ladies will allow me the pleasure of escorting you about the village, I will repay the kindness by ordering a nuncheon for us at the inn. I believe I saw a tolerable-looking place just at the top of the high street."

"Famous!" Dinah declared, her exquisite face glowing with joy at the prospect. "I promise you, my heart is quite aflutter at the very chance of an outing."

Honor wanted to scream. She hated to disoblige the girl, who had already suffered one severe disappointment at her hands, but she could not go with her to the village. Honor had no money for shopping excursions, and she certainly could not have the bills sent to Edmond. He was not her husband; never mind that he thought he was. And once he discovered the deception, he would be justified in expecting repayment for every groat he had expended.

No longer naive about the ways of the world, Honor knew that where women were concerned, men expected to be granted favors for their expenditures. Even before she had been offered a *carte blanche* by the detestable Jerome Wade, Esquire, she had known that fact. And though the idea of being in the barrister's debt quite turned her stomach, the thought of being in that same situation with Edmond caused an ache deep inside her heart. Though why it should be so, she could not say.

A silence seemed to have fallen upon the room as the other three inhabitants waited for her answer. Unable to think of a way to refuse without disappointing Dinah, Honor capitulated. "I shall be at your disposal," she said.

Having committed herself to the outing, Honor hoped fervently that a fresh snowfall would put an end to the plan, for barring help from the heavens, she would be obliged to think of a way to appear to shop without going so far as to actually leave the establishments with any purchases. With that thought in mind, she excused herself, saying she had correspondence that needed attention. "For if we are to go to the village, I shall certainly wish to post a letter to town."

The heavens failed to grant Honor's wish for bad weather, and she woke to beautiful sunshine streaming through her bedchamber windows. Someone had come in earlier to open the curtains, an act that had done nothing to disturb her slumber, and the morning was well advanced before she forced herself from the comforting arms of Morpheus. Owing to the two nights she had cared for Edmond during his illness, nights in which she had lain upon her cot for only brief periods of time, she had been exhausted. As well, she had stayed up quite late last evening, composing a letter to Uncle Wesley.

Choosing just the right words, she explained to her uncle that she had lost her job at Mrs. Bascomb's and that she was presently staying with Lady Raleigh and her daughter, recent acquaintances who had invited her for a few days' visit. Keeping the fib to its bare bones, inventing just enough to allay any fears her uncle might have for her safety, she asked him to see if the agency had another opening for her, a place where she might go directly from Raleigh Park.

The letter written, Honor had fallen into a deep and untroubled sleep. She might have remained thus until afternoon if Celia had not burst into the bedchamber, giggling like the child she was, and bearing a tray containing a plate of buttered muffins and a pot of hot, fragrant chocolate. She set the tray on the bedside table, then poured chocolate from a gentian blue teapot into a matching cup.

"Mmm," Honor crooned, stretching until every muscle in her body was alert before sitting up and taking the cup from Celia's hand. "That smells wonderful. Almost worth waking up for."

"I were that afraid you would be up and about before I returned." The words only just out of her mouth, the child gasped, then clamped her hand over her mouth as though to keep from revealing a secret.

Wondering at the maid's behavior, Honor sipped the sweet liquid, noticing as she did so that Celia's apron was askew, as if it had been donned hastily, and that a thick braid had escaped from beneath her mobcap, revealing hair as orange as a newly dug carrot.

"Did you go some place special?" she asked, the question one of politeness rather than real curiosity.

"No, ma'am!" Looking stricken, Celia hurried to the clothespress and began setting out fresh underthings. "I didn't go nowhere. I was just talking, I were. You know what a prattle-box I be. Don't pay me no attention. No attention at all."

Not wishing to pry into something that was, after all, none of her business, Honor took the easy route and put the matter from her mind. It was only much later, after she and Dinah had returned from their trip to Abbingdon, that the significance of Celia's slip became clear. For the moment, however, it seemed a matter of little importance.

The Inn of The Two Swans was a three-story building set well back from the street to allow for the changing of horses in the inn yard. Like the cottages on the outskirts of the little market town of Abbingdon, the inn was washed yellow, with a thatched roof and weathered oak doors and shutters. Lady Raleigh's coachman turned the barouche into the inn yard, then he held the spirited bays in check while the gentleman assisted the ladies to alight.

Leaving the coachman to see to the temporary stabling of the horses, Mr. Avery led Honor and Dinah toward the shops, entertaining them the entire way with his commentary upon the current extremes of dress employed by the London pinks.

"La, sir," Dinah said, "I vow I cannot credit half of what you say."

Placing his hand over his heart, as though mortally wounded, the gentleman said, "I am cut to the quick, Miss Moseby, that you should doubt my veracity."

The young lady blushed charmingly. "But, sir. To dye one's poodle and one's hair the same color! It goes beyond credibility."

"It goes beyond sanity," he said affably. "But there is much about the dandy set that defies belief." Then, with a warm look, "When you come to town for your come-out, I hope you will allow me to be the first to drive you in the park, to prove to you that I speak none but the truth."

The young lady's only answer was the heightened color of her satiny cheeks.

As they traveled up one side of Abbingdon's high street and down the other, it seemed to Honor that she had been given two unpleasant tasks to perform. The first, to try on every hat, shawl, and glove Dinah brought to her notice, and find some small flaw in each item that rendered it unsuitable for purchase. The second, and far more difficult task, was to play gooseberry to Dinah and Mr. Avery.

If they had been any other couple, Honor would not have minded in the least playing chaperon. She might even have rejoiced in their budding interest in one another. But they were not some other couple. They were Edmond's fiancé and his best friend, and for Edmond's sake, Honor must try what she could to keep the two apart. Not an easy task by any means, for Simon Avery was proving even more charming than he had been last evening.

Unfortunately, the gentleman's delightful manners were the least of Honor's worries. What bothered her most were the long looks he gave the girl when he thought no one was watching. Those subtle glances struck fear in Honor's breast. And as if that was not enough, she observed that each attention, each softly spoken comment gave new animation to Dinah's face and brought a sparkle to her green eyes.

Honor felt as though a giant hand were squeezing the very lifeblood from her heart. *Please,* she prayed silently, *do not let them destroy Edmond's happiness. Let Dinah find Mr. Avery's compliments and his flattering attention distasteful. And let him discover that charming little sprinkle of freckles across her nose and take her in disgust.*

"There is Madame Elise's millinery," Dinah said, locking her arm through Honor's and practically pulling the reluctant shopper toward the display window at the front of the single-story building. "Oh, look. Is that not a charming confection?"

Ashamed of herself for her silent plea to heaven for assistance, Honor followed Dinah's lead and admired the display. A simple rosewood settle had been placed in the window of the little shop and was cunningly draped with ell upon ell of poppy red satin, upon which had been sprinkled dozens of white feathers—mostly ostrich, but a few grebe—and in the midst of the riot of color sat one bonnet, a simple dark green velvet with a wide poke and long satin ribbons meant to tie beneath m'lady's chin.

Noting Honor's absorption with the display, Simon Avery said, "The bonnet would look smashing on you, ma'am."

"No, no." Honor shook her head so fast her own bonnet—her favorite before Edmond had tumbled her into his bed at the inn and crushed the hat beneath her—very nearly fell off. She was obliged to disengage her arm from Dinah's in order to straighten the offending item. "I never wear that particular shade of green," she explained. "But you must try it, Dinah, for it would be vastly becoming to you."

Happy to fall in with this request, the young girl led the way into the shop and asked immediately if Madame Elise would show her the hat in the window.

"*Mais oui, mademoiselle.*"

The milliner stretched her hand toward a pair of small tables, each equipped with a looking glass. "If you will please to be seated, I should be delighted to serve you."

Dinah took her place, removing the soft-crowned Coburg bonnet that matched her French gray pelisse and setting it upon the table. "And for my friend," she said, "something to compliment her eyes. Not that anything could equal them, of course. Such a beautiful dark blue. Do you not agree, Mr. Avery?"

The gentleman bowed, acknowledging the truth of the statement. "Of a certainty, Miss Moseby. With the exception of your own lovely orbs, I have never beheld eyes quite so striking. In fact," he continued, "Edmond and I were discussing that very subject last evening, after you ladies had retired for the night."

Honor stared at the man. Surely, this was more of his foolishness. She did not believe Edmond had ever looked at her long enough to notice the color of her eyes. To her amazement, Mr. Avery promptly disabused her of that misconception.

"If I remember correctly," he said, "Edmond likened the blue to a lake we both knew in the Peninsular. Surprised me, I can tell you, for I did not know the fellow could wax so poetic." An enigmatic smile played upon the gentleman's lips. "But you must ask him to repeat the observation, ma'am. Kind of thing ladies like to hear."

Feeling slightly breathless at the idea of Edmond speaking poetically about her eyes, Honor sat down at the table, watching absently as the milliner went to the back of the shop, where she opened the doors to a tall, glass-fronted case. Inside the case were at least a dozen wire forms, shaped to resemble a head, neck, and shoulders, and upon each form reposed a hat, each one more beautiful than its neighbor.

When the woman returned, she carried a Dutch bonnet covered in palest blue moire silk.

"Please to bare your head," Madame Elise said.

Knowing she should refuse, but unable to resist, Honor removed her brown bonnet and replaced it with the blue, allowing the milliner to tie the ribbons for her and adjust the long blue feather so it curled against her cheek. The effect was so wondrous it rendered Honor speechless.

"*Voilà!*" Madame declared, kissing her fingers for emphasis. *Très ravissant*."

"Oh," Dinah said. "You must have it, for I declare it is perfection."

"Rather," agreed Mr. Avery.

"There is a matching muff," Madame informed her. "Lined in softest white velvet. Shall I fetch it for you?"

Honor shook her head. "I think not."

Knowing that she could no more afford the bonnet than she could afford the numerous items she had been shown at the draper's shop, she untied the ribbons and handed the creation back to the milliner. "I find I do not care for it. Not that it is not lovely," she added quickly, lest she insult the woman.

Far from being insulted, Madame Elise smiled pleasantly and walked over to the counter where she placed the confection inside a waiting bandbox, packing tissue paper all around it to protect the long feather. The task finished, she left the bandbox on the counter and returned to the customers. "May I show you anything else?" she asked hope-fully.

Honor had already retied the strings of her brown bon-net and risen from the table. "I think not, thank you."

They remained in the shop only long enough for Dinah to purchase the green velvet and inform Madame where it was to be delivered. As they stepped back out onto the street, Mr. Avery consulted a handsome gold timepiece.

"I ordered our nuncheon for quarter past," he said, "so if you ladies have had enough shopping for the moment, I suggest we return to the inn."

By common consent they turned and strolled to the top of the street and The Two Swans. The building boasted two doors; the one on the left led to the taproom, while the one on the right gave access to the inn proper. It was through the door to the right that Mr. Avery escorted the ladies, stopping just inside the small entryway.

No sooner were they inside, than the proprietor, Ezra Givany, a round-bellied man of some sixty summers came from behind his desk to greet them with all due condescen-sion, smiling and bowing as if in the presence of royalty. "Sir," he said, "you'll find everything in order. The private parlor is waiting, likewise the room you booked so the ladies could get shed of their coats and bonnets."

"Excellent," Mr. Avery said, slipping his hand inside his coat and withdrawing a guinea, which quickly found a home inside Givany's leather smock.

After motioning to the thin, sparrow of a woman in an apron and cap who stood near the narrow wooden stairs that led to the upper floors, the man returned his attention to Mr. Avery. "Here is my rib, sir. She'll show the ladies upstairs."

Honor took a moment to hand over her letter for inclu-sion in the next London-bound mail, then she and Dinah followed the innkeeper's wife up to the room. Once they had refreshed themselves, they returned belowstairs to find the proprietor waiting to show them to the private parlor. So busy were they listening to the man's effusive assurances as to their enjoyment of the coming meal, they were inside the room before Honor had time to notice that Mr. Avery was not alone.

Edmond stood before the roaring fire. With his elbow propped against the wooden mantelpiece and one booted foot resting upon the brass fender, he gave his attention to his friend, who spoke of the new barouche he was having built for the Four-in-Hand Club's spring trip.

"Should be a jolly trip to Salt Hill," Mr. Avery said. "Will you be joining us?"

Whatever Edmond's reply, Honor heard only the timbre of his voice; the rich, deep tone, still slightly husky from his illness, seemed at one with the warmth of the flames in the fireplace. He appeared calm, his body relaxed, yet she sensed that the calm was an illusion, that he waited, alert, for someone or something.

When he saw her, he pushed away from the mantel, moving toward her with an effortless grace that caused a gentle flutter inside her rib cage. He smiled, and the flutter became a wild pulsating so disturbing she was obliged to remind herself that he was betrothed to Dinah, and that *she* had no claim upon him and had better stop responding to him as though she did.

"Ah," he said, as though he had been awaiting her arrival, "you are here at last."

Not knowing how she was to answer the remark, she countered with, "*I* am here, sir, but why are you? I understood you were to accompany your bailiff for a view of the estate. Have you discovered the whole in so short a time?"

"No, madam. As it turned out, my bailiff was laid upon

his bed with an ague, so I came to discover what my wife had found to interest her in the village." He looked her over. "Since I detect no additions to your wardrobe, am I to assume you found nothing to tempt you? Can it be that you are too discriminating in your tastes for provincial shops?"

"Acquit me, sir. I found enough to please any lady, but I was, perhaps, not in the mood for shopping."

Edmond's brows lifted, feigning shock. "Not in the mood for shopping? Madam, you are truly an original."

Honor felt herself blush to the roots of her hair. "Nothing of the sort. I am quite ordinary, I assure you."

"Ordinary? I cannot allow it to be so." Lowering his voice so that he would not be overheard by the others, he said, "You are a riddle, madam. One I have yet to solve." Catching her hand, he lifted it to his lips and pressed a slow, warm kiss upon each knuckle. "But I shall solve it," he said. Then he raised his head and looked directly into her eyes. "You may be certain I shall solve it, for I find myself curious to know everything about you."

Pulling her hand from his, Honor took a step back, afraid Edmond could hear the riotous thumping inside her chest. She told herself that her heart's rapid pace was a result of his thinly veiled threat to get to the bottom of her story, but deep within—in that part of her that no woman can deny—Honor knew her accelerated heartbeat was in response to those slow, tantalizing kisses and the feel of his lips against her skin.

Thankfully, Edmond seemed not to notice her distress and asked quite calmly if he might offer her a glass of sherry. Honor cared little for wine, but she nodded her assent, happy for any excuse that would prompt him to move away, anything that would end his unsettling nearness long enough for her to regain her composure.

She watched him walk across the garishly carpeted

room to a sturdy pine buffet upon which reposed a decanter and several crystal wineglasses, and after he poured small amounts of the red-brown liquid into two glasses, he returned to her. By that time she was herself again, though when she took the glass he offered, she was careful not to let her fingers touch his.

Taking a small sip of the nutty-flavored wine, she vowed to retain control of her wayward emotions, to be mistress of herself and the situation. However, as soon as Edmond led her to the small square table set for four, seating her so that he was to her right and Mr. Avery to her left, she realized she was in control of nothing. She had avoided the touch of Edmond's fingers, and now, due to the smallness of the table and the largeness of the gentleman, the slightest movement on her part put her in contact with him.

She sighed, for touching him was unavoidable. Inescapable.

Nor did Edmond contribute to her peace. Far from it. As though he were truly her husband, he took such liberties as must make any woman markedly uncomfortable. If he wished to offer some comment to Mr. Avery, the task necessitated draping his arm across the back of Honor's chair—an occurrence that happened more than once. And when she chanced to glance at the little enameled watch pinned at the front of her dress, he went so far as to lean over and whisper in her ear.

"Bored already?" he asked. And though the question was innocuous enough, the implied intimacy of a public whisper, not to mention the caressing warmth of his breath so close to her ear, sent her emotions soaring.

As for what was left of her composure, it all but deserted her when she chanced to look at him and discovered a smile of pure devilment in his eyes. *The cad! He is teasing me, and enjoying my discomfort!*

"Allow me to serve you a slice of ham," he said, his voice low and seductive.

Unable to speak, she merely nodded, and as luck would have it, just as he reached over to set the meat upon her plate, she reached forward to move her glass out of harm's way. It was inevitable that his arm should brush against hers. Not wanting to make a scene, however, she forbore the contact until he moved away, offering a serving of meat to Dinah.

Hoping no one noticed her lack of manners in not holding up her end of the conversation, Honor concentrated upon her meal, putting minuscule bites of something—she had little cognizance of what—into her mouth and swallowing, occasionally uttering monosyllabic responses to such comments as were put forward by Dinah or Mr. Avery.

Thinking she was managing admirably, Honor was about to congratulate herself when Edmond chanced to shift his long legs. Suddenly, she felt his muscular thigh flush against her knees, and though he moved away instantly, the awareness of him remained, almost as if he had left his imprint upon her.

After that, each time he moved, she felt it. And to keep herself from flinching, or doing something equally foolish, she was obliged to pay especially close attention to what was being said by her companions. Though, in all honesty, if her life had depended upon it, she could not have said what topic was being discussed.

For the duration of the meal, Honor kept her ankles crossed and her feet well beneath her chair. As much as possible, she rested her hands in her lap, and when she lifted her fork, she was careful to keep her arm close to her side. Anything to avoid touching Edmond.

Still, she was painfully aware of him—of his presence—for she could not stop her senses. She could no more prevent herself from breathing in the tangy aroma of his shaving soap, than she could cease to hear the smooth rhythm of his breathing.

One thing only could she control, and that was her eyes. Yet even they betrayed her, for once when Edmond was listening to Dinah's account of a book of poems she wished to procure from the subscription library, Honor ventured a quick glance at him. He was in profile, and though she had an unimpeded view of his dark brows, his strong aristocratic nose, and his angular chin, her traitorous eyes saw only his mouth.

It was a mouth worthy of study, for even though it appeared almost uncompromising in its strength and determination, his lips looked incredibly sensitive and responsive. Gazing at those lips caused a yearning inside Honor, a longing as old as time, yet somehow new and unnerving. Unbidden, the memory returned of the kisses he had pressed upon her knuckles, and recalling the feel of his warm lips upon her skin, she knew a desire to feel their firmness upon her mouth.

Stop this! Stop it now, before it goes too far.

Honor balled her hands into fists, until her fingernails dug into the soft flesh of her palms. *I cannot let myself entertain these thoughts about Edmond. He is Dinah's intended.* Furthermore, honesty compelled her to admit that even if he were not betrothed—even if there were no Dinah Moseby—Edmond would still be beyond her touch.

Honor knew the ways of society. Had her mother not learned to her heart's anguish the lesson of marrying above her station? Edmond Lawrence was a gentleman of family, wealth, and social standing, and such men did not marry the Honor Danforth's of this world. They might flirt with them. They might even steal a kiss if the opportunity presented itself. And if they suspected the lady would agree to it, they might offer a carte blanche. But they never offered their hand in marriage.

Facing the unpalatable truth of her ineligibility for a man like Edmond was a sobering experience, but it enabled Honor to relax her clenched fists, letting the fingers go limp in her lap. She had only just regained control of her emotions when Mr. Avery inadvertently set her senses reeling once again.

"By the bye, Edmond," his friend said, "speaking of poetry, I happened to mention to the ladies how you had compared your wife's eyes to that lake in the Peninsular. I could not remember just how you had said the thing, of course, so I suggested they apply to you."

Honor very nearly choked on the tea she had just sipped, and put the cup down quickly, before she sloshed the hot, fragrant liquid all over herself. Unable to credit her ears, she stared at the speaker, praying that Edmond would refuse to discuss the lake, and offer instead to toss his lifelong comrade into it.

Unfortunately, Edmond said nothing, and Mr. Avery failed utterly to discern Honor's displeasure, continuing his importuning. "Go ahead, old boy, tell your wife how the blue of the sky cast its reflection upon the calm, shaded water."

"Another time," he said, seemingly not at all put out of countenance. Then, with a smile, he turned to Honor, who added three cubes of sugar to her already sweetened tea, stirring with such concentration as must accompany the mixing of lifesaving herbs. "I shall be happy to tell you," he said softly. "You may tell me when."

Chapter 9

To Honor's everlasting gratitude, the innkeeper choose that exact moment to enter the room to inquire if everything was to the gentlemen's satisfaction.

"Quite," Mr. Avery replied. "A fine repast, Givany."

Edmond added his own agreement; whereupon, the innkeeper said, "If I may be permitted, sir, I should like to say how happy we all are to see you take up residence at the Park."

"Thank you, Givany."

In the background Mr. Avery murmured under his breath, "Here it comes, old man. Remember our wager."

Edmond chose to ignore his friend, giving his attention to the innkeeper.

"Not that we don't all miss Sir Frederick," Givany said, "for we do. As fine a gentleman as ever was, and well liked by all his neighbors."

"You knew him well, did you?"

"Aye, that I did, sir. Knew Mr. Carlton Lawrence as well."

Edmond seemed surprised to hear this. "You were acquainted with my father?"

"Oh, yes, sir. He was often at the Park when he was a lad, and time out of mind I chanced upon him and Sir

Frederick in the woods, playing soldiers, or out on the moors, hiding in one of the shepherd's huts, cutting up a lark of some kind." The innkeeper paused to let the information sink in. "In fact, Mr. Carlton stopped in at the inn when last he visited Abbingdon."

The innkeeper rested his arms upon his sizable stomach. "You were with him at that time, sir. Still in short coats, you were. And if you'll forgive the impertinence, already fair to being a fine lad, as anyone privileged to meet you could see."

Simon Avery smothered a laugh.

After a few more sycophantic observations about young Master Edmond, the innkeeper bowed himself out of the room, and the instant the door was closed, Mr. Avery let out a whoop. "Pay up, old boy, for you have lost the wager! Not but what I warned you how it would be. Before you know it, every villager over the age of forty will claim to remember something embarrassing you did or said when you were still a lad. It's their way of lording it over a fellow, putting him in his place, so to speak."

He turned to Dinah. "Edmond never lived in the country, don't you know, and when I was so obliging as to give him a few pointers on how it would be, he questioned my knowledge."

"But it is true," Dinah said, looking at Edmond for only a moment before returning her attention to Mr. Avery. "One cannot escape it. I declare I cannot go any place in Kent without one old tabby or another informing the entire company that she remembers when I was but a skinny child, never to be seen without dirt on my smock or scabs upon my elbows. It is quite lowering, I assure you."

"Isn't it just," Avery agreed. "I told Edmond he had much to learn about country life, especially that part in which everyone knows everyone else's business."

Edmond took the loss of the wager in good part, and since it appeared that everyone had finished the meal, he reached inside his coat for his pocketbook. "I collect, Cousin Dinah, that I should have sought advice from you first, before accepting a wager from Captain Sharp there. In the future, I will not be such a flat as to let him bamboozle me into risking the ready."

Avery laughed again and held out his hand. "Never mind about sharps and flats, old man. I believe twenty pounds was the amount agreed upon."

While Edmond searched for the proper denominations from among the rather thick stack of blunt in his pocketbook, he noticed a piece of folded paper that had been lodged between the notes fall to the carpeted floor, coming to rest just beneath the hem of the tablecloth. Though he had every intention of recovering the item once they all rose from the table, for the moment he ignored it, concentrating instead upon placing the twenty pounds in his friend's hand.

Busy countering some foolish comment from Avery, Edmond very nearly did not hear Honor's quick intake of breath. In fact, since she covered the gasp by coughing softly into her napkin, he might not have given the incident a second thought had her subsequent actions not been so bizarre.

After patting her lips with her napkin, she did not return the linen to her lap, as she pretended, but rather surreptitiously dropped it to the floor. It was only through careful schooling of his responses that Edmond managed not to turn and stare when she bent down and scooped up both the napkin and the piece of folded paper.

Keeping his thoughts to himself, he rose from the table and held Honor's chair, helping her to rise. To his further surprise, while he listened with an appearance of interest in Avery's chatter, Honor ambled over to the fireplace, pretending an interest in a rather mundane copy of the popular Staffordshire pitcher commemorating the famous meeting between the boxing champion, Tom Cribb, and the American black, Tom Molineaux.

Apparently having looked her fill of the two indistinct faces on the ceramic pitcher, Honor turned her back to the hearth, her hands behind her. Just before she moved away, she tossed a small, wadded paper into the fireplace.

"What a very pleasant outing this has been," she said much too cheerfully. "I thank you, Mr. Avery, for thinking of it."

Avery made her a bow. "My pleasure, ma'am. And if it pleases you, while you ladies retrieve your wraps and bonnets, I shall settle up with Givany and wait for you at his desk."

"Very well, sir. We shall be but a few moments."

Edmond waited only until the ladies were on the stairs, then he hurried back inside the private parlor, walking straight to the fireplace. As good fortune would have it, Honor's aim was no better than her attempt at subterfuge, for the paper had hit the corner of the firebox and bounced back to land safely just beneath the fender.

It was the work of a moment to reclaim the paper, unfold, and read it. It took considerably longer, however, to comprehend the significance of the rather detailed catalog of money spent at the inn in Upper Chidderton. There was a shilling here, a half-crown there, with the largest expenditure listed being two crowns given to one John Trogdon for the purchase of shaving soap and a razor.

Edmond shook his head in bewilderment. The whole added up to mere fiddler's money. Why should anyone even bother to record such trifling amounts?

More baffling still, why should such an insipid list inspire Honor to take covert measures to keep it a secret? Try as he might, Edmond could discern no logical reason why she had felt compelled to destroy the paper. There was, of course, the matter of the vowels written at the bottom of the page, but that, too, represented such a small amount. Surely, Honor did not believe he would come the ugly over paying her expenses at the inn; after all, she was taking care of him during his illness. Were the amount one hundred times five pounds, he would not have protested.

Wanting to understand, he read through the whole a second time, paying special attention to the neatly written lines at the bottom of the paper. *Mr. Lawrence, IOU the sum of five pounds. I have your card and will repay the money when I return to London. Honor.*

No last name, and no address. Obviously, she did not mean for him to be able to locate her in the future. But why? Odd, surely, for a woman who claimed to be his wife.

His wife. Of course. No sooner had the thought entered his head than he knew why she had not wanted him to see the paper. It proved that they were not married. Because a husband was legally responsible for his spouse's debts, no wife would write such a vowel. Naturally, he already knew they were not wed; what was significant was that *she* had no way of knowing that he knew.

Hearing the ladies coming down the stairs, he put the paper back where it had resided these past few days and joined Avery in the entryway. Curious, Edmond thought, that the more he learned of Honor, the more of an enigma she became.

The solving of the puzzle was still uppermost in Edmond's mind when the shopping party returned home later that afternoon. "What kept you?" he asked when

Simon Avery finally strolled into the wainscoted library. "I have been home this hour and more."

"We took a little drive. Dinah . . . I mean to say, Miss Moseby . . . showed us a bit of the moors."

"Oh." His thoughts otherwise, Edmond lifted a book off the shelves, glanced at it idly, then shoved it back into place, annoyed that it did not distract him from his contemplation of Honor and the note she tried to destroy.

"Our luck was out, though," Mr. Avery continued, "for the road was still far too muddy from the melting snow, and we were obliged to turn back before we saw even one of the famous wild ponies. Spotted a few sheep and a tumbledown hut or two, but other than that it was all just a vast expanse of moorland rising to rocky tors. Impressive enough scenery in its way, but I think I prefer Kent."

"There is, of course, no accounting for taste," Edmond muttered.

Not at all offended, Mr. Avery pulled a chair near enough to the cozy fire to enjoy its warmth, while at the same time propping his feet upon a corner of the slightly abused oak writing desk. His booted ankles crossed, he leaned back in a relaxed manner, his hands cradling the back of his head. "From your greeting just now, I collect you were worried about us. Or perhaps not *all* of us," he suggested.

Refusing to rise to the bait, Edmond abandoned the books on the shelf and walked over to the desk, perching on the edge and turning slightly so he faced his friend. "Before we left the inn, did you notice how Honor went over to stand in front of the fire?"

"Can't say I did, old boy."

Mr. Avery became aware of a mark on the toe of his left boot, and lifted it for closer inspection. "Would you look at that? I had these top boots from Hoby less than a fortnight ago, and already there is a great scratch. I should not be at all surprised if my man threatens to leave my service over this, for he is forever telling me about some duke whose valet is about to retire, and—"

"Cut line," Edmond said, retrieving the folded note from his pocket and tossing it so it landed in the gentleman's lap. "Read that, and tell me what you think."

After a quick perusal, Mr. Avery said, "I think your . . . er, 'wife' . . . has a head for details."

Edmond chose to ignore the irrelevant remark. "Did you read her vowels?"

"I did." He tossed the note onto the desk. "I find nothing so strange about it. Probably saw some geegaw she wanted and had not the ready to stand the nonsense. You do not begrudge her a trifle or two, do you? I know you told me last evening that she was not really your wife, but when I think of the gelt you dropped on that opera dancer you had in tow for scarcely more than a weekend—"

"Do not be an ass! The circumstances are not at all the same."

"Of course they are not. Your wife—"

"Devil take it! Stop calling her that."

"Then what would you have me call her? A fellow cannot go around calling a lady by a name she has not given him permission to use."

Edmond ran his hands through his hair, not knowing what else to do with them or his frustration. "That is just the point."

"What is? Demmed if you aren't talking in riddles today, old boy."

"Honor. She is a lady."

Mr. Avery swore. "Naturally she is a lady. Never known you to be such a cloth head. One has only to look at her to know what she is. Intelligent, educated, modest, and pretty-behaved, she has all the refinement of a gentle-woman, as any but a fool would see."

Edmond nodded. Concentrating on the slight marring of the boot his friend had bid him notice earlier, he said, "Now, of course, it seems absurd to me that I could ever have believed her an adventuress bent upon extorting money from me."

"Quite absurd," replied the Job's comforter.

"In retrospect, I think the suspicion had more to do with the laudanum I had been given than to any real evidence of duplicity on Honor's part."

"And the laudanum has finally worn off?" Mr. Avery asked dryly.

This time Edmond swore. "Must you rub salt in the wound?"

"A thousand pardons. Just wanted to be certain I had the facts straight. So you no longer suspect her of anything?"

"Of nothing dishonest, at any rate."

Picking up the paper, Edmond read it again, as if he did not already know it by rote. "If I needed any proof of her honesty—which I do not—this paper would be sufficient, for it shows that she had access to my pocketbook while I was still ill and out of my head. She could have taken every last groat at any time, and I would have been none the wiser."

"That she could have," Mr. Avery replied. "Instead, she *borrowed* five pounds."

"And means to repay it. But why? For what purpose would a lady need five pounds? A thousand pounds I could understand. But five? If I could find that piece to the puzzle, I might discover the answer to several other questions."

"Such as?"

"For one thing, who is she? For another, what was she doing in the wilds of Devon, alone and with nothing but a valise in hand? And finally, why did she pretend to be my wife?"

"Here is a thought," Mr. Avery said sarcastically. "Why not ask her?"

Edmond shook his head. "Like a fool, I promised not to. Besides, I do not think she would tell me."

"Ma'am," Celia said, rising from the stool she had pulled up before the bedchamber window in order to make use of what remained of the afternoon light. Having dropped a polite curtsy, the maid clutched to her chest the sewing she had been working on, waiting and watching while her mistress surveyed the room—a room liberally strewn with shawls, gloves, stockings, handkerchiefs, and ribbons, as well as several ells of material in woolen, silk, and dimity.

Still wearing her redingote and bonnet, Honor looked about her at the disarray. The ells of material she had never seen before, but she recognized the other articles without the least difficulty. And why should she not? Had she not tried on each of them earlier in the day, as she and Dinah had made their way from shop to shop? Tried them on and refused them every one.

As if walking in her sleep, she approached the bed, knowing even before she lifted the lid of the lone bandbox what she would find beneath the tissue paper. Neatly packed to avoid damage to the delicate ostrich feather was the moire silk Dutch bonnet Madame Elise had personally tied beneath Honor's chin.

"The little muff be beneath the hat," Celia said, her voice hushed with excitement. "Such a cunning little thing, ma'am. Fashioned of palest blue it be, like the sky, and lined in velvet white as new snow."

When Honor said nothing, the young girl approached the bed and timidly stroked one of the ells of material, a dark blue merino. "Mr. Lawrence give me leave to choose the colors I thought'd best suit you, on account of you telling him I were a talented seamstress." The girl blushed at the words she repeated.

"When?" Honor only just managed to whisper.

"This morning, it were."

Wondering why she had dismissed the incident before, Honor remembered the girl's giggles when she brought the chocolate, and her wish to keep something a secret.

"You be still abed when Mr. Lawrence drove me in to the village. It were just him and me in Sir Frederick's gig, and so polite he treated me, I couldn't hardly believe it. Asking were I warm enough, and did I need a rug over my lap."

Celia sighed at the recollection. "Nobody never treated me so fine before. And while Mr. Lawrence went to talk with the shopkeepers about putting your purchases on his account, and making sure they delivered 'em prompt like, he left me at the draper's to pick out the material for your dresses."

Suddenly, the child's pale face turned bright red. "I were almost to the draper's door when Mr. Lawrence called to me. 'Celia,' he said, 'long as you picking out materials, you might as well get a piece for yourself.' I near fell over in a swoon, not knowing what to say. Then Mr. Lawrence said I were to get a real nice piece, on account of he were sure that were what my mistress would want me to do."

Tears filled the young girl's eyes. "'Cept for my uni-

form, I ain't never had a dress that weren't worn by somebody else first."

Honor stood beside the bed, her hands balled into fists,
embarrassment and anger fighting for dominance inside
her. She longed to scream her frustration; to tell the maid
to pack up every last item and take them back to the village that very minute, or barring that, toss them out the
window. But the words remained unsaid, imprisoned
painfully inside her throat. Who but a monster could look
into that child's face and spoil her joy?

*I ain't never had a dress that weren't worn by somebody
else first.* The words still ringing in her ears, Honor swallowed what was left of her own pride. "What color did
you choose for yourself?" she asked.

"Green, ma'am. On account of my carrot hair."

"When next you go to your room, you must bring it
down and let me see it."

The girl bobbed a curtsy. "You want I should show you
the drawers and petticoat I already got cut out for you
today?"

Honor shook her head. "Not now, thank you. At the
moment I find myself in need of some fresh air. I think I
will take a walk while it is still light." Having made the
decision, she turned and hurried to the bedchamber door.
"And, Celia?" she said, just before she stepped outside the
room.

"Yes, ma'am?"

"While I am gone, I would appreciate it if you would
put all these things away."

"Away, ma'am?"

"Yes. In the clothespress. Back in the boxes. I leave the
decision to you. I just do not wish to see the . . . er . . . dis-
order when I return."

The young girl blinked. "You want I should put all of

'em away, ma'am? Even the pretty cream shawl with the gold fringe? I were meaning to press it so you could wear it at dinner tonight. It would look real nice with the rose sarcenet."

"No," Honor said, "put everything away. Every last item."

It was two very disparate people who met on the gravel path where it curved around the greenhouses. One of the walkers, having traversed the entire length of the path from the main house, past the three connected green-houses, and over a hill to the apple orchard, was retracing his steps. He strolled quietly, calmly, lost in thought, in contrast to the other walker who took quick, agitated steps, laboring all the while to control her anger. Their one common bond was the accident of having chosen the same walk, although the coincidence was not remarkable, since the melting snow had left the ground a quagmire and made any other path inadvisable.

For Edmond's part, though he appeared calm, the mild physical exercise had not proven as beneficial as he had hoped. Far from clearing his brain and affording him the answers he sought, the quiet stroll had served only to raise another question.

While he had stood quietly, staring beyond the dozen or so rows of leafless apple trees, he had been reminded of a chance remark he had chosen to ignore yesterday, a re-mark he now found unsettling in the extreme. It con-cerned a message the landlord's wife at the inn at Upper Chidderton had given Edmond. The message was meant for *his* wife, to inform her of the availability of another bedchamber, in case she still wanted that extra room she had requested when they first arrived.

Too caught up in his own thoughts at that time, Edmond had ignored the significance of Honor's having requested separate rooms from the first. Now, of course, with him no longer deluded by his own idiotic assumption that she was an adventuress who had somehow lured him to the inn with the sole purpose of stealing his money, the incident took on a whole new meaning. Obviously, it had never been any part of Honor's plan to share his room, and that she had done so was a result of necessity rather than design.

Not for the first time, he cursed his foolishness for having gotten so inebriated he let himself be put in a post chaise bound for Devon. Looking about him for something that would relieve his frustration, he picked up a small stone, aimed at one of the apple trees, and threw with all his strength. It was an empty gesture, for when the stone hit the tree, it did little more than dislodge a small clump of frozen snow trapped in the bend of one of the branches. It did nothing at all to ease his feelings of being an unwitting pawn in a game played by the fates.

He swore. The entire fiasco was beginning to make sense to him. Unfortunately, with each new piece of information gained, he found Honor's actions more excusable and his own more reprehensible.

For some reason—a reason Honor did not wish to divulge—she had been stranded by the storm. Then, somehow, her fate had become inextricably linked with his. Probably she had stopped to give him aid at the accident site. A good Samaritan.

Whatever the circumstances, they led to the two of them sharing the only available room at the inn. Sharing it for two nights.

Here, then, was a logical explanation for why Honor had chosen not to sign her full name to the vowels, nor to indicate how Edmond might find her once she returned to

London. She had wanted to remain anonymous. Fate had compelled her to spend two nights alone with a man, compromising her past all reclamation, yet she retained a hope of escaping the situation—and the man—with her reputation intact.

When Edmond woke from his laudanum-induced sleep, Honor was trying to get away; not with his money, as he had supposed, but with her anonymity. It all seemed quite clear now. Her valise was packed, and she was dressed for the out of doors. If he had been asleep, as she thought him, she would have escaped, and he would never have known anything more about her than that she had the most beautiful blue eyes he had ever seen.

But she had not escaped. He had stopped her. Not for any benefit to her, but for his own purposes—to help him avoid being compromised into marrying his cousin's stepdaughter. It was Edmond's fault entirely that Honor was here with him, for he had forced her to come.

A fine way to repay her for nursing him through his illness!

Since she had kept her identity a secret from him, was still keeping it a secret, it probably meant she had not given up her plan to get away should an opportunity present itself. What she did not understand was that there was no escaping now. Not when he knew her to be a lady—a lady he had surely compromised.

In a situation of this type, there was but one course open to a man of principle—parson's mousetrap. Somehow he must convert their bogus marriage into a real one, with the fewest possible number of people being apprised of the true circumstances. It was the only honorable thing to do.

Not that he expected Honor to see it his way. Though she had proven herself to be a practical person, a person who made the best of a bad bargain, she was also a woman who knew her own mind. Had he not already locked horns with her over the simple matter of the purchase of a few wardrobe necessities?

Of course, he had found a way to get around that objection. Now he must devise a plan to assist him in what he felt certain would be an even more difficult task—convincing Honor that marriage was their only alternative.

As he retraced his steps, he was so lost in trying to think of a workable plan that he failed to notice the sound of quick footsteps approaching. As well, his view of the path was obstructed by the three connected greenhouses, buildings where smoke billowed from each of the three chimneys and where the glass in the windows was frosted over as a result of the cold outside and the heat on the inside. When Edmond rounded the curve in the path, he careened into a body both shorter and noticeably softer than his own, a body that was propelled backward immediately upon impact."

"Oomph!" Honor gasped as she collided with a wall of immoveable masculinity. Before she knew what had happened, she found herself sitting upon the damp path, her bonnet knocked completely off her head and her skirts tossed about, revealing an embarrassing amount of shins and knees.

Before she had time to straighten her skirt, or even to notice the hardness of the gravel beneath her, she was being lifted to her feet and supported by arms that felt almost as hard as her landing place.

"Are you hurt?" he asked, "I cannot tell you how sorry I am. I—"

"Let me go," she ordered, pushing Edmond's hands away and stepping back a pace. Embarrassment intensified her anger, making her speak more sharply than she had intended, and once the floodgates were open, she could not hold back the tide of her indignation. "Have you not humiliated me enough for one day? Must you maul me about as well?"

"Maul you about?"

Startled by the unexpected verbal attack, Edmond stared at her. Anger warmed her cheeks, and fire sparkled in her magnificent eyes, making him want to do the very thing he was about to deny ever having done. "When have I ever mauled—"

He paused in his declaration of innocence, suddenly recalling having tumbled her into his bed only the day before. It had been a surprisingly enjoyable tumble, if he remembered correctly, one in which he had been sorely tempted to kiss her soft lips. She had turned away at the last moment, but he had found himself fascinated by her earlobe, nipping it softly, then following that pleasurable taste with little kisses, working his way back toward her mouth. Of course, he had not actually thought of it as mauling her about, but he could see how she might deem it so.

As for humiliating her, however, he was jolly well innocent of that charge!

"You are an overbearing man!" she said, her breath coming in short gasps that made it impossible for him not to notice the rise and fall of her well-shaped bosom.

"But I assure you, I—"

"I knew how it would be the instant I set eyes upon you. Handsome men are always spoiled."

Handsome? That was encouraging. Obviously she was not as immune to him as she would have him believe.

"But you are more than spoiled," she continued. "Being in the military must have given you a taste for power, for once you decide upon a thing, you give the order, fully expecting those order to be obeyed."

"No, really, you misunderst—"

"You care not one whit for anyone else's feelings."

"I must protest, for I care a great deal what—"

"No! You care for nothing but getting your own way." She gulped a rather ragged breath. "If you possessed even one iota of human compassion, you would never . . . would not have . . . "

Unaccustomed to being railed at, he was about to give her a well-deserved set down, when he noticed that the anger that had lent such vivid color to her cheeks had suddenly ebbed, leaving her face pale.

"You . . . you should not have . . . you had no right to . . ." Her voice caught and she paused, swallowing several times in an attempt to regain her control.

Never a man to be swayed by feminine dramatics, Edmond surprised himself by reaching out and catching her by the shoulders, then slowly pulling her against his chest, enfolding her in his arms, wanting to soothe away whatever had upset her. To his further surprise, she did not pull away, but let him hold her close.

Ignoring all her quite unflattering observations regarding his character, Edmond concentrated on the accusation that seemed to have unleashed the flood of her anger. "How have I humiliated you?" he asked softly, resting his chin against the top of her head. "Tell me, so that I may make amends."

"The clothes," she said, her voice still unsteady. "You knew I did not want them. Yet you went against my wishes."

As if to assure herself that he was paying heed to her words, Honor pushed against his chest with her hands, freeing herself enough to allow her to raise her face and look into his. "Every human being, no matter how rich or poor, truly owns but one thing—their own body. And as the owner, they are not obliged to acquiesce to anyone's wishes but their own. They have the right to say no. And no one, great or small, may take that right away. To do so is to strip a person of their humanity."

Edmond listened to the simple statement and knew a moment of regret. "I acted without thinking," he said, "and I apologize."

As he looked into her upturned face, he noted a wary— almost frightened—look in her eyes. And though he did not excuse in the least his own thoughtlessness, he knew with a certainty that he had never put that wariness there. His actions might have been the last straw that triggered her outburst, but she was not the least bit afraid of him. Never had been!

So, he thought, the words Honor had uttered were meant for someone else—someone who had tried to force her to his will. She had said *no,* and that person—it had to be a man—had ignored her wishes. And if Edmond was any judge, she still perceived that man as a threat. Which, of course, answered part of the question of why she was in Devon, alone and unprotected.

Unprepared for the red-hot anger that shot through him at the thought that anyone should dare cut up Honor's peace, he slipped his hand to the side of her neck, touching his thumb to her chin so that she could not avoid his gaze. "Who has dared to strip you of your humanity?"

She tried to look away, and though he did not restrain her, he put enough pressure beneath her chin to encourage her to remain as she was. "Tell me," he said. "And I promise you he will never bother you again."

Chapter 10

Edmond waited for an answer, but Honor merely closed her eyes so that he could not see the battle being waged inside her.

"Please," he said, "tell me. I can protect you."

Honor felt the strength of Edmond's arms as he held her close, the security of his broad chest, and she longed to surrender, to give herself into his keeping. Yet she dare not. Jerome Wade was a dangerous man, possibly even deranged, and she would not allow Edmond to become a target for his anger. Edmond believed himself to be her husband, and as such, he felt obliged to protect her. But she would not let him risk his own safety.

"You . . . you are mistaken," she said. "There is no one. I—"

"Honor," he said, his voice so soft it was a mere whisper, "I will not let anyone hurt you."

She could feel the warmth emanating from his body, smell the faint spicy scent of his shaving soap, and she wondered how it would feel to have the right to be protected by such a man. To be loved by such a man.

While she pondered that question, his hand moved ever so slightly against her neck. The tips of his long fingers touched the fine hairs at the base of her skull, sending delicious shivers all the way to her knees and making them unaccountably weak.

Succumbing to an impulse as old as time, she leaned her entire weight against his firm body. And to her surprise, he seemed to know just what she wanted, holding her so close she forgot to breathe. Despite the thickness of their coats, she was acutely aware of his physical strength, a strength that was at the same time frightening and reassuring.

"Honor," he said, his voice muffled, his lips pressed against her hair.

When he spoke her name, that weakness assailed her knees again, and she wondered how it would feel to have his lips pressed not against her hair, but against her mouth.

Even before her mind had formed the question, her body sought the answer. And despite the warmth of embarrassment that stole up her neck at her brazenness, she turned her face up to his.

For what seemed a long time, Edmond remained quite still, his gaze searching her eyes. Honor's breathing seemed to stop as she waited for him to find what he was looking for. Whatever it was, he must have found it, for slowly he bent his face to hers and gently, softly brushed her lips with his own, the touch so tender Honor thought her heart would shatter into pieces from the wonder of it.

Unable to stop herself, she pressed even closer to him, and as she did so, she felt a shudder run through him. Then he tightened his arms around her, the gentleness of a moment ago replaced by an urgency that prompted her to slip her arms around his waist.

Lost in the wonder of what was happening to her, Honor tried to draw even closer, only to have Edmond suddenly grasp her by the shoulders, forcing her away from him.

After the warmth of his nearness, the air seemed bitterly cold against her face. She was about to protest his desertion when she heard a door close just behind her.

"Hello!" Lady Raleigh said, surprise in her voice. "Have you come to see my flowers?"

Where Honor's face had been cold before, now it was aflame with mortification. If her life had depended upon it, she could not have answered Rowina's question, for speech was impossible, almost as impossible as standing without the support of Edmond's arms.

Obviously, he labored under no such handicap, for he answered pleasantly, "We would very much like to see your flowers. That is, if you would not find it a dead bore to explain the whole to a man who cannot discern a rose from a daisy."

Rowina Raleigh laughed charmingly. "That is one of the joys of flowers, Cousin. One need not be an expert to appreciate their exquisite beauty and fragrance. One hesitates to paraphrase the Bard, but a rose would smell as sweet even if you mistook it for a daisy."

Opening the door she had just closed, she said, "Please. Let me show you my treasures."

As though visiting the greenhouses had been their primary reason for traversing the path, Edmond held the door for Honor, then followed the two ladies inside the warm, moist enclosure.

"You may wish to remove your wraps," Rowina suggested, divesting herself of her own gray wool pelisse and hanging it from a peg beside the door. "The temperature inside each of the greenhouses is as near tropical as Eames and I can make it."

Having said this, she motioned toward a large pile of old rags stacked on a little stool at the far end of the enclosure, and to Honor's astonishment, the rags suddenly

stood upright, turning into a wizened little man of unde-
cipherable years. "That is Eames," she said. "He came
with me from Kent when I married Frederick, and he is
the only person I trust with my plants."

The man's wrinkled face was very nearly the color of
the earthen pots seen all about the place, and out of that
face peered eyes of a startling blue-gray. By the time
Honor had recovered from the surprise of those eyes, the
little man had lifted his billed cap in respect, then scurried away to one of the adjoining greenhouses.

Following Lady Raleigh's advice, Honor gave her
redingote to Edmond, and while he hung both their coats
on the peg, she looked around her, her interest piqued in
spite of her earlier embarrassment. Never before having
been inside a greenhouse, she was surprised to discover
just how much flora the small building held. Every square
inch was utilized, with some plants growing from beds in
the ground, while others were arranged in various-sized
clay pots placed upon row after row of tiered benches.

At the far end of the building was a screened fireplace, and as Honor looked at the blazing fire, Rowina
apologized for the heat. "In this particular greenhouse,
Eames keeps the fire going at all times. As well, those
iron kettles you see in each corner hold peat fires, and
are never allowed to go out."

"Whew," Honor remarked, fanning her face with her
hand. "Eames does a very good job. I do not believe I
have ever been quite so warm. Or so damp."

Rowina pointed to a system of narrow copper flumes
that began in the ceiling and circled the walls, then me-
andered through the beds in the ground. "The water is
warmed first, then allowed to trickle through holes so
small one must stand quite close to see them. The plants

in here are tropical, and they must have both ample heat and water."

Rowina called to their attention something particularly interesting about each plant, and if they asked, she supplied the names, both Latin and common. Many were in bloom, and even those not showing flowers displayed beautiful leaves or fronds. Honor found most interesting the plants that grew upon other plants or on rocks, some even dangling in clusters from a piece of wood, all gathering their sustenance not from the soil but from the air.

Breathing in the warm, moist perfume, Honor said, "The fragrance is heavenly. How marvelous you must find it, Lady Raleigh, to be among such beauty every day. Such a fascinating pursuit."

"Yes," she agreed. "But lest you perceive the greenhouses to be nothing more than the expensive toy of an indulged dilettante, perhaps I should inform you that the other two houses are maintained for the sole purpose of growing herbs."

"Herbs? Do you mean condiments?"

She smiled kindly, as if explaining something to one whose knowledge was understandably limited. "Mine are medicinal herbs. These particular plants are far too difficult and costly to gather in their native habitant, so I tend them here, then harvest them for a laboratory in London. Of course, I have no way of knowing their full potential, for many of their healing properties have only just begun to be uncovered by our learned scientists." She lowered her lashes, almost as if embarrassed to have divulged this information. "However, I am pleased to have even so small a part in something of such value to mankind."

Honor turned to Edmond, who stared at the delicate

blonde before them, surprise writ plainly upon his face. "I had no idea," she said, "had you?"

Edmond shook his head. "I had not." To Rowina, he said, "Madame, such an important project must not be discontinued."

Rowina Raleigh nodded. "My kind, generous Frederick understood the importance of my work, and that is why he went to such expense to have these greenhouses constructed for me. My place in Kent was nothing to it, I assure you."

She paused for a moment, and when she spoke again, her voice had lost its usual calm. "Now that you understand my life's work, Cousin, I hope you can forgive me for having acted—shall we say, precipitously—in the matter of putting forward a possible union between yourself and Dinah. It was selfish of me, I know, but I so hated the thought of removing from Raleigh Park and abandoning my wonderful greenhouses. And since the child must surely wed one day, it seemed a perfect solution."

Dinah had never been betrothed to Edmond! The information lifted a weight from Honor's heart. Edmond was free to love where he chose; not, of course, that she expected him to choose her. Still . . .

"Naturally," Rowina continued, a gentle smile upon her face, "once I met your lovely wife, I knew the two of you were meant for one another." Turning to pinch a spent blossom from a succulent stem, she said, "You will forgive a mother her misguided machinations?"

"Think nothing of it," Edmond said. "For who could fault a parent for wishing to see her child well established? As for abandoning the greenhouses and the herbs, that must not happen. Let us put our heads together after dinner, ma'am. Surely, there is some workable solution to this dilemma."

*   *   *

As it transpired, the workable solution involved more than the putting together of their two heads, and for the next four days, Honor saw almost nothing of Edmond. When he was not riding about the estate with his bailiff, getting acquainted with his land and his tenants, he was in town, conferring with Abbingdon's only solicitor. "A man," Edmond said, "noticeably short on common sense and long on pomposity."

Of course, Honor was quite happy that Edmond was from home for most of the day, for that way she need not converse with him, or even look at him, if she did not wish to. And she definitely did not wish to. Not after the way he had kissed her. And especially not after the way she had responded!

For the two days following their embrace, she had reminded herself hourly to exercise caution around him. To be polite, but distant. Otherwise, she was much afraid she risked falling in love with him, a circumstance guaranteed to break her heart.

Now, however, four days after the kiss, Honor felt she could look at Edmond without fear of embarrassing herself. She had, she felt certain, recovered completely from the madness that had possessed her while on the gravel path.

It was after one particularly long and work-filled day, when Edmond entered the drawing room where the three ladies and Mr. Avery had gathered for a game of cribbage following the evening meal, that Honor was forced to admit to herself that the madness was still upon her. Edmond had but to enter the room to set her pulses racing. One look at him, and all her pretensions to sanity and level-headedness disappeared like the morning fog.

Because of his late return, he was still dressed in a riding coat of corbeau green worn over biscuit-colored breeches. His brown hair was rakishly windblown, and traces of mud showed on his once glossy top boots. Yet to Honor he appeared even more handsome in this relaxed attire than when dressed in his fancy evening clothes, a situation that caused a noticeable flutter in the region of her heart.

"So, you are returned at last," Mr. Avery said. "We were beginning to think you had wandered onto the moors and become lost."

Edmond bowed to the ladies. "My apologies for appearing in all my dirt."

"Please," Lady Raleigh said, "think nothing of it. This is your home, after all. If you may not be relaxed here, then where?"

He sketched her another bow before collapsing into the closest chair, his long legs stretched out in front of him. "There is so much more to be learned than I had ever dreamed possible."

"Your bailiff knows his business, then?" Mr. Avery asked.

Edmond nodded. "To my everlasting gratitude. For I begin to suspect that estates do not run themselves, as a number of our more profligate acquaintances would have us believe. My cousin was an admirable man, but his absence has been felt over the past months. And, of course, that idiot of a solicitor is of no use whatever."

Honor, wishing she could ease the lines of fatigue around Edmond's mouth, asked if she might pour him a glass of wine.

"I should much rather you kept me company while I ate. I asked Traverchick to see what he could do about having something sustaining sent to the dining room, for I have eaten nothing since just after daybreak."

Inordinately pleased that he sought her company, Honor felt herself blush from head to toe, and hoped that no one was close enough to notice her reaction. Not that they would find much to marvel at; believing her to be a new bride, they would think nothing of her apparent pleasure in wishing for a few moments of privacy with her husband.

She, on the other hand, knew she ought to be more circumspect. However, she needed some time alone with Edmond, to discover for herself if their kiss had been but a moment's pleasure taken and then forgotten, or if it had touched his heart and soul as it had touched hers. It was something she had to know before she risked making a complete fool of herself.

By the time the butler came to inform Edmond that his dinner was served, Honor had managed to control her foolish emotions and was able to take his proffered arm with what she hoped was an air of detachment.

When they were alone in the corridor, just outside the dining room, she said, "You look tired, sir."

"And you," he said, looking her over and noting the new cream shawl, "look lovely." He lifted several strands of the silk fringe, letting them slip through his fingers. "Thank you for wearing this."

Not wanting to reveal the pleasure his words gave her, she lifted the skirt of her rose sarcenet an inch and thrust the toe of a gold slipper forward to his notice. "Do not, I pray you, pay me compliments, for as you can see, once I forsook my boots, it was the work of a moment to abandon my scruples entirely."

Edmond chuckled. "I cannot credit it to be so, ma'am."

"Oh, but it is. My principles are by now quite unreclaimable. In fact, you may count yourself fortunate, sir, if when next I visit the shops, I do not discover an opera cloak lined in Russian sable. Or, perhaps a diamond tiara I cannot live without."

"I am not worried," he said. "Do you think I could be in your company for this entire week and not know you to be a lady worthy of her name?"

What she would have answered to this rather breath-robbing question, Honor was never to know, for at just that moment the knocker sounded on the front door.

"Whoever can be visiting at this hour?" Edmond asked. Then, motioning to the butler, who stood waiting to usher them into the dining room, he said, "See who it is, Traverchick. It must be important for anyone to call so late."

By mutual consent, they waited in the corridor while the butler did as he was bid. And though Edmond could not immediately see who stood on the other side of the partially open door, he listened to the exchange.

"Yes?" Traverchick said.

"I am looking for Mr. Lawrence."

From the voice, Edmond judged the caller to be a gentleman in his middle years.

"Please give him my card, and ask him if I may have a moment of his time. The matter is quite important."

Before the caller had finished his statement, Honor gasped. Without saying a word, she snatched her hand from Edmond's arm and ran toward the entryway, practically pushing the butler aside in her haste to pull the door open wide. At sight of the slight gentleman with the hint of gray in his temples, dressed in a modest greatcoat and curly brim beaver, she uttered a cry and threw herself upon his chest.

"Uncle Wesley!"

"Honor, girl," the man said, his voice thick with emotion. "Thanks be to heaven. I have found you at last."

Chapter 11

For just a moment, when Honor gasped, it had crossed Edmond's mind that the person at the door might be the man she feared. Another second, however, and that thought vanished, as she threw herself at the gentleman, hugging him as though she meant never to let him go.

"Uncle Wesley," she said, stepping back at last and pulling the gentleman inside so Traverchick could close the door. "How ever did you get here?"

"'Tis a long and tedious story, my girl. And quite frankly, I would as soon hear the one you have to tell."

"Of course you would," Edmond said, walking forward, his hand extended in greeting, "but perhaps it is a story best told in a bit more privacy than the vestibule can provide."

The gentleman took the proffered hand, but his grip was of short duration and anything but friendly. "I am Wesley Coverdale," he said, his tone icy. "Honor's uncle."

"And I am Edmond Lawrence. I have not yet had my evening meal, and was about to enter the dining room when you arrived. May I invite you to join me, sir?"

Mr. Coverdale's eyes, though almost as dark a blue as his niece's, held none of the warmth, and at the moment they cast daggers at the man before him. "I did not come for food, Mr. Lawrence; I came to find my niece."

"And I perceive that the search has filled you with anxiety. But if you would suspend your anger for a short while, sir, and join me in the dining room, I am certain I can explain everything to your satisfaction."

The more Edmond talked, the more the visitor looked as though he wished he had brought a pistol. Without taking his eyes off Edmond, he said very quietly, "Fetch your coat, Honor. I have a post chaise waiting outside to take us back to the inn at Abbingdon."

"No!" Edmond said. Then, noting the older man's rising anger, added, "You had much better come into the dining room, sir, before the others hear us and come to investigate."

"Others? What others?"

"My cousin, Lady Raleigh, and her daughter."

Surprise was writ plainly upon the gentleman's face. "There are *ladies* here?"

"I sent you a letter, Uncle, about me being here with Lady Raleigh and Dinah. Did you not get it?"

He shook his head. "No, my dear. I received no letter. When your trunk arrived, and you were not with it, I nearly went out of my mind with worry. I waited for two days, days in which I feared . . . But never mind all that, you must know what I suspected. On the third day I bought a ticket for the stagecoach to Lower Chidderton and went straight to Bascomb Manor."

Honor lowered her gaze, focusing on the lapel of her uncle's greatcoat. "So you met Mrs. Bascomb. I suppose she told you what happened. Why . . . why I left."

"It is irrelevant what she told me. Suffice it to say, it is a miracle I did not murder that harpy right there in her overstuffed drawing room."

To Edmond's surprise, the suggestion of murder prompted Honor to throw her arms around the gentleman's neck once again. "Best of uncles," she said, tears dampening her eyes.

"Here now, none of that," Mr. Coverdale said, reaching inside his coat and withdrawing a handkerchief.

Edmond expected him to hand the linen to Honor to dry her tears, but, in fact, he used it to wipe something from his own eyes. After blowing his nose rather noisily, he returned the handkerchief to his pocket, then looked at Edmond as if to take his measure. "I have just one question for you," he said.

"And I shall answer that and any others, sir. But please, let Traverchick get your bags and send the post chaise on its way."

"Yes, Uncle, please. We need not go right away. Tomorrow is ample time."

That last remark startled Edmond into an oath, though he quickly covered it. "Nothing should be decided on an empty stomach, sir. Please. Stay the night, at least."

Looking from Edmond to his niece, Mr. Coverdale was persuaded to relinquish the services of the post chaise. "Let me but take care of the postboy, then I will return."

While he was outside paying off the chaise, Honor asked Traverchick if he would have Celia bring a tray of tea and toast to her room. "For my uncle cannot eat heavily at night. His is a stressful stomach."

"I quite understand, madam. I shall inform Celia, then have a room prepared for the gentleman."

"Thank you."

Turning to Edmond, she said, "It would be best if I met with my uncle alone."

Edmond reached for her hand, taking it in both of his. "Are you quite certain?"

"Quite. He has been worried for my sake, and it would be unkind not to ease his mind as quickly as possible. We can speak more freely in my chamber."

Edmond suspected the gentleman's fear had something to do with the unknown man whose existence so distressed Honor, but since she had not taken Edmond into her confidence, he had no choice but to acquiesce to her wish for privacy. Unable to do more, he gave her hand a squeeze, then released it. "It shall be as you wish. At least for tonight. But I beg you will inform Mr. Coverdale that I am at his disposal at any time tomorrow. If there are questions he wishes to ask me, I shall do all in my power to answer them."

"So," Wesley Coverdale said, his tone as frosty as the early morning air, "you are telling me that you do not, after all, suffer from a loss of memory."

"No, sir. I do not."

"My niece is under the impression that you lost your memory as a result of a coaching accident. Is she mistaken, as well, in believing that you think she is your wife?"

"I am not married, nor have I ever believed myself to be so. As for your niece, she is not so much mistaken as misled." At the gentleman's indrawn breath, Edmond hurried to say, "The fault is mine entirely, but before you call me out, I beg you will let me explain how this entire fiasco began."

Wesley Coverdale's reply was lost in the necessity of controlling his horse—or more correctly, Lady Raleigh's chestnut mare, Bright Star—for the beast took exception to a startled partridge that sounded its hoarse *kee-ah,* then took wing, its rust-colored tail feathers vivid against the cloudless blue sky.

Though the sun shone brightly, the air was quite crisp, and the breath of both men and horses was visible. As they paused at the top of a knoll Edmond had traversed for the first time just the day before, he looked off into the distance to a patch of fallow acreage and the centuries-old, yellow-washed cottage that accompanied the land, both land and cottage untenanted since his cousin's death.

"It wants a tenant," he said when his guest followed his gaze to the cottage. "There is much I need to learn about the proper handling of an estate this size, but I do not believe the task is beyond my comprehension."

"I collect, then, that you mean to concern yourself in the welfare of the property."

"I mean to do more than that. This is my home now, and I wish to pass it down to my children and their children. As far as I am concerned, I could be happy if I never set foot off the place again.

"Of course," he added quietly, glancing briefly at Mr. Coverdale, to gauge his reaction, "Honor will want to visit London from time to time, to see you and her friends. And it is my hope that you will visit us often, as well."

"So. The wind lies in that quarter, does it?"

Edmond did not answer right away. "You may not believe this, sir, but I am not totally without principles. I know Honor has been compromised, and I am prepared to make her my wife. Furthermore, I promise you that she will be treated with the kindness and respect due her. My only concern is how the marriage may best be done, without apprising those here at the Park that we were not actually wed when we first arrived. I suppose we must return to London so the ceremony can be performed in the bride's parish."

Mr. Coverdale's face showed little enthusiasm. "Before you dash to the stables and hitch a team to your traveling chaise, I should like to back up just a bit, for I have heard nothing of your feelings for my niece. Do you love her?"

Edmond was taken aback by the question. He had not supposed that love played a very large role in the business of marriage, and he certainly had not expected to hear such a query from a solicitor. Settlements, dowries, pen money, those were the subjects he was prepared to discuss.

"I admire her. I respect her. I like her. And I am prepared to spend my life with her. Does that answer your question?"

"Yes," the older man replied, his voice flat. "I suppose it does."

"Good. Then I have your permission to pay my addresses to your niece?"

"You do not need my permission. Honor is four and twenty, and well able to decide for herself what she should do."

Edmond had asked the question as a show of respect. It was a mere formality. Nevertheless, to ask it made the betrothal seem more conventional and less an act of necessity.

"However," Wesley Coverdale said, interrupting Edmond's thoughts, "just so we understand one another, I wish you to know this. If it were within my power to say you yea or nay, I would say nay. And should Honor come to me for advice upon the matter, that will by my answer to her."

Edmond could not have been more surprised if the

man had turned and spit in his face. "You would with-hold your permission?"

"If it were within my power. Yes, I would."

"But why?"

"Because, Mr. Lawrence, I want more for my niece than marriage to a man whose principal reason for the union lies in his wish to do the right thing. And unless I miss my guess, Honor's answer will be the same."

"As you say, sir, that is only your guess."

"True. In the event that I am mistaken, and Honor decides to accept your hand, there is something more I wish you to know."

"And that is?"

Mr. Coverdale swallowed, and Edmond had the fleeting thought that the gentleman might be swallowing a rather large dose of pride. "I wish you to know, Lawrence, that Honor is more than just the niece of an obscure London solicitor. She is the granddaughter of Sir Harry and Lady Danforth, and though they have never deigned to acknowledge her, she is a Danforth nonetheless, and as such she is entitled to the respect due any lady. And if you ever forget that fact," he said, his blue eyes deadly serious, "I am prepared to blow a hole through your heart, if I swing from the gibbet for my pains."

Far from being insulted by the threat, Edmond was impressed by the man's devotion to his niece. As for her being a member of the gentry, that mattered none at all to him. Not now, at any rate. Not for some time.

"I hesitate to contradict you, sir, but I feel certain that Honor's being a lady has little to do with her grandparents and everything to do with the gentleman who reared her. And should I ever forget even one of her wonderful qualities, you have my permission to shoot me with one of my own pistols."

Wesley Coverdale chuckled. "Then we understand one another."

"We do, sir."

The air pretty well cleared between them, the two gentlemen turned their horses and returned to the house. It was while they strolled up from the stable that they encountered Lady Raleigh, who had just spent an hour in the greenhouse.

"Well met, Cousin," Edmond said. "I imagine the servants have apprised you of the fact that Honor's uncle arrived last evening. Allow me to make him known to you."

Edmond was beginning to despair of ever getting Honor alone long enough to make his proposal, when he received assistance from an unexpected source. The entire company was enjoying tea and cakes in the drawing room, with Rowina Raleigh explaining to an interested Mr. Coverdale her passion for growing things.

"Of course, there are often disappointments," she said, "times when no matter how one tries, a plant just will not make the adjustment from its native environment to the imitation world of the greenhouse. But the joys far outweigh the sad moments. In fact, it is my belief that gardening forces one to accept life and death, and reminds one to live in the present. Otherwise, those rare and all-too-fleeting moments of beauty would be missed. Some of those beauties come overnight and linger for only a day, and if we are not watchful and ready to appreciate and enjoy the miracle heaven has given us, we may never get the chance again."

"I see, Lady Raleigh, that you have cultivated more than just flowers. You have acquired a philosophy that many a verbose cleric would envy."

Rowina blushed prettily. "You are very kind, Mr. Coverdale. Perhaps you would care to see my flowers."

"I should deem it a privilege, ma'am. And since your philosophy suggests the seizing of the day, may I be allowed to see them this afternoon? Perhaps after this lovely tea?"

"It would be my pleasure, sir."

"And perhaps," he added, "Mr. Avery and Miss Moseby would care to accompany us." He looked pointedly at Edmond. "I understand you gave my niece and Mr. Lawrence a tour just yesterday, so I shall not ask them to come along."

"No," Edmond said, quick to accept the gentleman's assistance in getting his niece alone, "I had a book I wanted to show Honor, a rather rare edition I discovered in the library. She and I will entertain ourselves indoors while you nature lovers enjoy a tour of the greenhouses."

What Honor thought of such an arrangement of her afternoon neither her uncle nor Edmond saw fit to ask. If they had, they would have discovered that she was not averse to spending an hour alone with Edmond, especially since she expected to be returning to London within a matter of days. And once she left Raleigh Park, she had no expectations of ever seeing him again—a circumstance that left her feeling decidedly down pin.

Last night she and her uncle had talked. Seated in the comfortable blue chairs, her bedroom fire blazing cozily, they had shared their stories. She explained to him the entire sequence of events, beginning with her fending off the unwanted advances of Mrs. Bascomb's nineteen-year-old nephew, and ending with her arrival at Raleigh Park, representing herself as Edmond's wife.

Her uncle heard her through, then after only a few

bites of toast and a sip or two of tea, he related his frantic search for her once he learned that Mrs. Bascomb had turned her out without furnishing her with so much as a ride into the village.

"Then, of course," he said, "when I discovered that you were not in Lower Chidderton, had not even been seen there, I very nearly panicked. Thank heaven someone finally told me there was an Upper Chidderton. I made haste to travel there, and you can imagine my dismay when the landlord of The Ram informed me that you were in the company of a handsome gentleman—a gentleman he believed to be your husband . . ."

Honor rested her hand on her uncle's arm. "You thought that Jerome Wade had somehow managed to find me."

"Yes. And that he had you in his power."

He fell silent, gazing into the orange and yellow flames. Wade is still having the house watched, for I have seen his man skulking about on more than one occasion."

Honor knew a moment of fear, a fear she realized she had not felt since coming to Raleigh Park with Edmond.

"If it was not for this ill-advised impersonation, my dear girl, I might have suggested that you remain here with Lady Raleigh. However, for her to be a proper chaperon, she would need to know the truth of your relationship to Mr. Lawrence, and once she discovered the deception, I am persuaded she would not wish to lend herself to a falsehood."

"No. I cannot think she would."

He sighed, as though grieved to choose an alternative neither of them liked. "Then we have only one choice; we must return to London and try to sneak you into the house until such time as new employment can be found for you. We can leave tomorrow."

Not wanting to examine why the suggestion felt like a knife driven through her heart, Honor had insisted they remain long enough for her uncle to recuperate from the rigors of his earlier journey. Two to three days had been settled upon as an appropriate time to depart, but now Honor was finding the thought of leaving far more difficult than she had imagined.

Waiting in the vestibule while the others fetched their wraps for the walk down to the greenhouses, Honor was forced to school her thoughts not to be forever recalling the day she had met Edmond in front of the greenhouses—the day he had held her in his arms and kissed her.

Bidding herself think of something else, she remained at the door until the other four were well on their way down the gravel path, then she returned to the drawing room where Edmond waited. "And now," she said, not really caring what excuse had served to enable her to remain inside with him, "where is that book you seem to think I would find of such interest?"

Edmond stood at the French windows that gave onto the wide expanse of front lawn. Snow still covered the grass, but the warm sun had melted all but minute traces of white from the branches of the elm trees off to the right.

"The book was a ruse," he said, turning and strolling toward the fireplace. "I needed an opportunity to speak with you alone."

"And to do so required subterfuge? Why? I cannot think that anyone in the household would remark our being alone."

Edmond smiled. "You are ever forthright, my dear. It

does seem rather foolish, I suppose. A bit like locking the stable doors after the horse has galloped away."

"Excuse me?"

"Especially foolish," he continued, "considering the many times we have been alone. Times, I might add, that were compromising in the extreme."

"Compromising to whom?"

"Why, to a young lady of sensitivity and breeding."

Honor had been standing, but now she perched on the arm of one of the sofas, a look of perplexity upon her face. "A lady of sensitivity and breeding? I must be rather a slowtop this morning. To whom do you refer?"

Edmond straightened his cravat. He had made a clumsy start of this proposal, and it was not going at all the way he had intended. "I refer to you, of course."

Honor's back was suddenly ramrod straight, and her chin had lifted in a manner that could only be called stubborn. "What did my uncle say to you?"

"Mr. Coverdale said nothing you would not like, I assure you."

"Then explain to me how a man can compromise his wife."

"Honor, please. We both know that you are not my wife, so let us—"

"He told you that? I cannot believe it of him. Uncle Wesley was never one to betray a confidence."

Edmond shook his head. "He did not. I already knew."

"You knew?"

Her voice was but a whisper, and though he would not have believed her back could become any straighter, somehow it did. "How long have you known?"

"Please," he said, "let us put the subject of my supposed memory loss aside for a moment."

"*Supposed?* Did I hear you correctly?"

Ignoring the question, he said, "What we need to discuss now is how we are to handle this situation so the fewest people know the full story."

She studied her hands where they rested on her slender thigh, the fingers interlocked. Her face was paler than he had ever seen it. "Uncle Wesley and I will be leaving for London soon—tomorrow, actually—so you may handle the *situation* by telling whatever story best suits your purpose."

"No! What I mean is, there is no point in your leaving. I have discussed it with Mr. Coverdale, and he has given his permission for me to pay my addresses. To beg your hand in marriage."

"Has he now? How odd. And quite unlike Uncle Wesley." Her tone was chillingly calm. "Tell me, if you will, which of you very proper gentlemen first mentioned the word *compromised*?"

"Does it matter?"

She did not answer, and Edmond almost wished someone would come into the room and interrupt this conversation. Somehow his well-rehearsed speech was not going as planned, and for the life of him, he could not think how to get it back on the right path. It was not as if he had ever proposed to anyone before, nor even thought of doing so. Without practice in such matters, surely a man might be forgiven a little gaucherie.

He looked at her pale, calm face. Damn it all! Could she not help him out a little here?

"When you asked my uncle's permission to beg for my hand, were those the words you used?"

Edmond tried to recall his exact words. All he remembered in particular was her uncle's threat to put a bullet through his heart, but he doubted she wanted to hear that. "I said something about how I respected you, and admired you."

"I see. Anything else?"

"Only that I was prepared to make you my wife. Is that not enough?"

If possible, her face turned even paler. "Quite enough," she said.

"And your answer?" he asked, a pulse suddenly pounding in his temples, like a bugler calling the troops to arms.

To his dismay she stood and walked to the door, and only when her hand touched the knob did she turn back to look at him. "Though I do not recall a specific question ever having been asked, I will, nonetheless, give you my answer. While I am conscious of the honor you do me, Mr. Lawrence, in being *prepared* to make me your wife, I find I must decline your offer."

If she had screamed obscenities at him, Edmond could not have been more surprised. "Decline?"

"Yes, sir."

"But why?"

"Why?" she asked, her voice maddeningly calm in the face of the tumult going on inside him. "Because I do not believe we would suit."

Edmond only just controlled his anger. "You refuse me? And all you offer by way of explanation is platitudes? 'We would not suit!' Deuce take it, Honor, have you nothing more to say than that?"

She raised her eyebrows, as if surprised by his question. "If I may borrow your own words, sir, is that not enough?"

"It jolly well is not enough. You know I—"

Leaving the room, Honor closed the door upon his words. Not caring who saw her, she lifted her skirt and sped up the stairs to her bedchamber, where she locked the door to the room, then dragged one of the blue chairs across the floor and pushed it against the dressing room door. When her privacy was assured, she threw herself upon the bed and let the heartache and the tears have their way.

Honor realized she must have cried herself to sleep, for when she awoke, the dimness of the room told her it was late afternoon.

"Ma'am?" Celia called through the door. "I can't get in."

It must have been the maid's voice that awakened her, that and the persistent knocking.

"Go away," she called.

Honor did not want anyone to see her. She did not cry often, had never been one of those women given to easy tears, but every time she succumbed to the necessity, she paid for it with a stuffed head and puffy eyes. Though what difference such trifles made now, when her heart was broken, she could not say.

If only Edmond had said he loved me.

He did not love her, of course. She knew that. But he might at least have given lip service to the conventions. The word might have acted as a balm to her broken heart.

Not that she would have married him no matter what he said. She loved him too much for that.

And she did love him. She could admit it now, now that she knew there was no hope for them. But her loving him was not enough. Had she not seen firsthand what happened when a woman adored a man to distraction—a man who did not return her feelings? She had watched her mother walk down such a path, and Honor had no intentions of repeating the error. Not even with Edmond.

Especially not with Edmond! She loved him too much to do that to him, or to herself.

The tears started again.

Celia knocked even harder, the sound fairly echoing inside Honor's head. "I'm that sorry, ma'am, but you got a letter. And the man what delivered it said the sender be waiting for an answer."

"A letter from whom?"

There was a pause. "I dunno, ma'am. I bain't able to read."

Ashamed to have forced the admission from the girl, Honor said, "Slide it under the door, Celia. And thank you."

Within seconds a sheet of ordinary paper materialized on the floor.

Honor could not imagine who would be sending her a letter. Of course, there was only one way to find out, and though she had no wish to think of anything save the ache in her chest, she remembered that Celia had said the writer was waiting for a reply.

Later, she told herself it was the stuffy head that made her so naive, but at that moment, all she could think of was that the letter must be important if it required an answer.

The moment she lifted the paper from the floor, she recognized the neat handwriting, and a shudder of revulsion ran through her. Instantly, she dropped the wafered sheet, as though it were a serpent, then scrubbed her fingers down the side of her dress.

Jerome Wade!

It seemed like hours before she was able to bend and pick up the paper a second time. Taking it over to the window to make use of the light, she tore open the wager and unfolded the single sheet. For a moment her fingers shook so badly she could not bring the words into focus. Finally, after several deep breaths, she steadied her hand enough to read the short missive.

Honor, My Love,

    Your uncle was from home when your letter arrived, so I took it upon myself to open it. It was very naughty of you to disappear without telling me. But now I know where you are, all is forgiven. I have come for you. I have procured a room at The Two Swans, and I will expect you there by nine of the clock this evening. If you should fail me, something quite unpleasant will befall your new friends.

                    Your adoring Jerome.

The lock played havoc with what was left of Honor's nerves, and she came very close to screaming. Thankfully, the door popped open before that happened, because she knew that if she let herself scream, there would be no stopping the sound.

Celia sat on the floor near the top of the staircase, and as soon as the door opened, she ran toward her mistress. "Oh, ma'am," she said, her child's face reflecting the fear in Honor's own. "Summit be wrong, I can tell."

"My uncle, Honor finally managed to say, "where is he?"

"He be still at the greenhouse with her ladyship."

"Please. Fetch him for me."

"Yes, ma'am." The girl was halfway down the stairs before she remembered she had not curtsied, and she turned to do so. "Excuse it, ma'am."

"Just go!" Honor said, more sharply than she had meant to.

Celia's hurried footsteps, plus the loud banging of the front door brought Edmond from the drawing room. "What the devil?" he said angrily. "Can a man find no peace in . . ." The words died on his lips as he turned to look up the stairs where Honor stood, trembling, a paper clutched in her hand.

"Honor?" he said, "what is it?"

Not waiting for her answer, he took the stairs two at a time until he was before her, his strong hands on her shoulders. Her face was ashen, and her beautiful eyes were red-rimmed and haunted. "What has happened?"

When she made no reply, he reached down and gently pried her fingers loose, taking the paper from her. After reading it through, he crumpled it into a wad and threw it across the landing.

Damn the bastard!

Filled with rage, Edmond longed to throttle the scoundrel. He craved to feel his fingers tighten around the man's throat, to squeeze the very last breath from his body. At the same time he wanted to take Honor in his arms, to comfort her, to assure her that he would fight heaven and hell to see that no one ever again put such fear in her eyes.

Frustration gnawed at him, for of the two things, he wanted most to hold Honor. Yet he could not do so. He had no right. Had she not told him less than two hours ago that she wanted no part of him?

"Damn that, too!" he said. Then he bent and lifted her in his arms, carrying her into her bedchamber, not stopping until he reached the chair that stood near the fireplace. Still holding her fast against his chest, he sat down, arranging her comfortably on his lap, and encouraging her with a gentle hand to her head to make use of his shoulder.

"Edmond," she said, "I . . ."

When her voice broke, he tightened his arms around her and laid his cheek against the top of her head. "Rest now," he whispered. "All will be well. I promise."

Her uncle found them thus when he entered the room several minutes later, his cheeks red from the cold and his breath coming in short gasps. He had run the entire way, and now, perceiving that she was in good hands, he felt decidedly *de trop*.

"Have I come upon a fool's errand?" he asked, the words punctuated with quick intakes of air.

Without turning around, Edmond said, "I dropped the letter somewhere on the floor. Read it. It is from the man who is terrorizing Honor. He has followed her here."

Wesley Coverdale swore. "The blackguard. I should have called him out months ago. I shall be obliged to do so now."

"No," Edmond said, "you will not. That pleasure will be mine."

Chapter 12

The next time Honor woke, a new day was beginning, and from behind the blue-and-silver hangings at the bedchamber window, she could detect the soft gray light of dawn giving way to morning sunlight. She could not remember getting into bed, nor even changing her clothes, yet somehow she was beneath the covers, dressed in her plain lawn nightrail with the ribbons tied snugly at the neck and sleeves.

The last thing she recalled was sitting before the fire with Uncle Wesley, sipping a cup of hot, fragrant tea sent up to her by Lady Raleigh. Suddenly suspicious, she sat up, only to have the room sway dizzily before her eyes. So. One of Rowina's soothing herbs had found its way into the tea.

Though she objected to being drugged, Honor supposed they had done what they thought best. She had certainly been in no condition yesterday to object. Not after reading Jerome Wade's letter. And though Edmond had been wonderful, holding her in his arms, and whispering comforting words into her ears, the fear brought on by the letter would not go away.

Now, with the coming of a new day, Honor knew the fear would have to be faced; otherwise, she might spend years running from a man whose obsession prompted him to believe he was entitled to direct her affections and her life. She would not do so! She had run long enough. Somehow, Jerome Wade must be stopped.

Needing to get up in order to clear her head so she could think logically, Honor threw back the covers and swung her feet over the side of the bed. At her movement, something or someone stirred on the far side of the room.

"Who is it?" she asked, her voice husky from sleep and nervousness."

"Shh. It is only me. Go back to sleep if you can."

Recognizing Edmond's voice, Honor snatched the covers back up over her, holding them close to her chin. "What are you doing in here?"

Avoiding her question, he rose from the blue chair, tossed aside a quilt that had been covering him, then raised his arms high above his head, as though he needed a good stretch. Because he was dressed only in breeches and a shirt, she could see the muscles bunch and relax in his broad chest as he stretched. Of his coat, cravat, and boots there was no evidence, and adding to the deshabille of slept-in clothing, his hair was mussed and a night's stubble showed on his face. He was, at that moment, the handsomest man Honor had ever seen, and she wished with all her heart that he would stretch his arms toward her and offer to hold her again.

But he made no such offer.

Bending to the fire, he poked at the banked coals, encouraging them to produce a small flame. "I rode over to the inn last night," he said, "after you were asleep. Wade was not there."

"Not there?" Honor relaxed her grip on the covers.

"Are you telling me it was all a hum? That the letter was some kind of cruel joke?"

"No, I am saying only that the blackguard was not there at that time." Edmond put the poker away, then leaned his back against the mantelpiece, looking not at Honor but at the light showing around the edges of the window hangings. "He was registered right enough, and his traps were there, but though I waited a full three hours, he still did not appear."

Honor did not know if she was more relieved or distressed by the news. She wanted Jerome Wade out of her life, but if Edmond had found the man, she knew they would have fought. And though Honor had no doubt that Edmond could defeat almost any man in a fair fight, she could not convince herself that the barrister understood the meaning of gentlemanly fair play.

She shivered, remembering one evening when Wade had come to see her uncle, using the pretext of discussing a trial whose defendant had been one of Wesley Coverdale's clients. Honor had served tea, and when her uncle had chanced to leave the room to find a written statement the barrister claimed he needed for the next day's trial, she had been obliged to make conversation.

Having met the slender blond man only once before, and unnerved by the intense way he looked at her—his cold gray eyes seeming to look beneath the layers of her clothing directly to her skin—she had found small talk difficult. Noticing the rather intricately carved wolf's head that formed the ivory handle of the walking stick he had not relinquished at the door, she commented upon the workmanship. Without a word Wade had pressed a button beneath the wolf's head, and faster than she could assimilate his intent, he had withdrawn a cunningly concealed sword from the hollow stick.

Horrified, Honor had gasped. The gleam in the man's eyes was more feral than that of any wolf. "Do not fear," he had said, his voice as cloyingly sweet as treacle, "I carry the weapon only for those who would cross me."

Recalling Jerome Wade's words, Honor shivered again. "The man is evil," she said, more to herself than to Edmond, who pushed away from the mantelpiece and strolled toward the dressing room door.

"I do not doubt it for a minute," he said. "That is why I do not wish you to be alone until such time as I can have a talk with him."

"A talk? Believe me, he will not listen to reason. I have tried."

For just an instant Honor detected an expression in Edmond's eyes she had never seen there before. A look that was, in its own way, as primal as that wolflike gleam of Jerome Wade's. "The man will listen to me," he said. "Depend upon it, I can be most persuasive."

After Edmond left her bedchamber, Honor scurried from beneath the covers and quickly washed and dressed herself, giving her long hair a cursory brushing before twisting it into a knot and pinning it atop her head. Feeling less vulnerable once she was decently attired, she went in search of something to eat.

"You are abroad early this morning," Lady Raleigh said from her place at the dining room table. "Please to take a seat, and allow me to serve you something from the sideboard."

While Honor did as she was bid, Rowina lifted each of the lids of the half dozen chafing dishes, announcing their contents even as their aromas wafted across the room. "With what may I tempt you? Braised eggs? Poached salmon?"

Honor breathed deeply. "Mmm. Some of everything, please, for I am ravenous. I seem to have slept through yesterday's dinner hour," she added meaningfully.

"Which is exactly what you needed," her companion replied unrepentant, "for sleep is the universal healer. I collect, however, that you wish to pull caps with me for having added one of my herbs to your tea."

"Certainly not, ma'am."

Rowina smiled. "Not even one very small cap?"

"Not one, for I am convinced you meant well."

"Ah, but there is the rub, is it not? People always *mean* well, and their good intentions rob us of the privilege of scolding them as we would like."

Effectively *robbed* of any lingering annoyance, Honor laughed. "I see you are wise to the ways of humankind."

"Not always," she said.

Selecting a particularly succulent-looking piece of fish, Rowina placed it on the plate, adding a *soupçon* of dill sauce. "In this instance, I had made Mr. Coverdale a tisane to calm his stomach, and he found the brew so soothing he asked if I knew a similar palliative that would help you sleep. Of course, I did. And since your uncle warned me you would not be pleased by what he called his interference, saying you had your own way of doing things, I am quite prepared to have you ring a peal over me, if that is your wish."

"But it is not my wish. How could it be, after you have been so kind as to see to my breakfast?"

After serving the plate with small portions of each of the remaining dishes, Rowina set it before Honor, then filled both their cups with steaming coffee.

She fell silent for a moment, then blushing added, "A very interesting man, is Mr. Coverdale. I wonder what the London ladies could have been thinking of to allow such a kind and thoughtful gentleman to slip through their fingers."

Though Honor had wondered that same thing many times in her life, to hear the question spoken by a lady of Rowina Raleigh's beauty and connections left her at a loss for words. As it turned out, the subject was forgotten immediately, as a commotion of some sort made itself heard from the kitchen region.

"Lawks!" a female shouted, her voice carrying as though she were in the next room. "We'll all be murdered in our beds!"

At the noise Lady Raleigh rose instantly. "What on earth can be the matter with Cook?"

Other voices, too muffled to be understood, were added to the din made by Celia's aunt Clara, and by the time Traverchick entered the dining room, his cravat pulled all askew by his hastily donned coat, Rowina was halfway to the door, ready to investigate the commotion.

"My lady," the butler said, his shoulders seemingly more stooped than usual, "it's Eames."

"Eames? What has happened? Is he injured in some way?"

"No, my lady. He's sore distressed, right enough, but the problem has something to do with the greenhouses. Near as I can make out, him gasping for breath the way he is from running up to the house, someone has been messing about the plants."

Watching Rowina push past the elderly butler and hurry toward the kitchen, Honor felt her stomach tie itself into a large knot. She recalled Jerome Wade's letter, and his threat that if she did not come to him at the inn, something unpleasant would befall her new friends. Somehow she knew that whatever had happened at the greenhouses, it would be his doing.

"Go get Mr. Lawrence," she told the butler.

Trusting him to obey her instructions, she sped down the corridor after Lady Raleigh. Hurrying past the linen room and through the servants' hall, where the half-empty plates on the long table gave evidence of a break-fast hastily abandoned by at least a dozen servants, she reached the kitchen only to discover that Rowina and the gardener had just left.

In their wake pandemonium reigned, for the cook had chosen to enact a Cheltenham drama, as if she, and not Eames, had discovered the trouble in the greenhouses. Having given way to hysteria, the woman was sprawled in a rocking chair conveniently near the massive stone fireplace, alternating between moaning and predicting dire happenings, while a frightened scullery maid waved burnt feathers beneath the older woman's nose. All around her, housemaids and abigails alike wrung their hands or merely stood about gawking, enjoying the un-expected excitement.

Paying no heed to the hysterical cook, or to Celia's plea for her to wait until she could fetch her a wrap of some kind, Honor ran outside and followed Rowina and the gardener down the gravel path, catching up with them just as they reached the greenhouses.

From the outside all appeared well, and Honor spared a moment to hope the excitement was all much ado about nothing, a hunt for a mare's nest. Unfortunately, she was forced to forsake the hope of a false alarm the instant she stepped into the warm, moist enclosure, for everything inside had been laid waste. It was as though the neat, organized greenhouse she had visited the day before had been a dream, while before her was the real-ity—a nightmare reality—of mud, broken pots, and mu-tilated plants.

While Honor looked about her at the destruction, the knot inside her stomach squeezed so tight it threatened to disgorge the few bites of food she had had time to swallow before Traverchick had appeared in the dining room. Someone had taken a scythe—the implement lay on the floor where it had been tossed aside once the deed was done—and cut, smashed, knocked over, or broken every item in the greenhouse. Not one clay pot remained whole. Each of the rows of tiered benches had been ruthlessly overturned, their precious cargo shattered on impact with the floor. Every last plant bed had been trampled under foot.

Honor looked about her, unable to believe the wanton vandalism, unprepared for the desolation she felt when first she glimpsed the misery on Rowina Raleigh's face. The lady's skin was ghostly white, and her green eyes were wide with shock and disbelief. Not a sound passed her lips. It was as though the blow was physical, and the wound too deep for mere words.

"Ma'am," Honor whispered. "I am so sorry."

Rowina seemed not to hear her, and after a time she turned and went through to the adjoining greenhouses. Honor had not the heart to accompany her, but waited helplessly for her to return. She was not gone above two or three minutes, and when she reappeared, her steps were slow and none-too-steady, the deliberate movement telling its own story of what had awaited her in the other two greenhouses.

By the time Edmond and Uncle Wesley arrived, one without his coat, the other missing both coat and cravat, Lady Raleigh and the gardener were on their knees, carefully sifting through the piles of soil, seeing what plants might be saved. Both their faces were streaked with tears.

Chapter 13

As long as she lived, Honor would never forget the anger she felt. The impotent rage. How could anyone commit such a mindless act?

"This was not your fault," Edmond said, stoking the drawing room fire with a vehemence that was at odds with his controlled words.

"No, it was not," Wesley Coverdale agreed.

Honor sat very erect, her chin held high. "I never thought it was. Nor will I dignify that cowardly act by claiming even an unwitting part in its commission. Jerome Wade destroyed those plants and herbs. He is a demented man, and though he is in the area because he has fixed upon me as the object of his desire, the sin is on his head. He will have to answer to heaven for it, not I. I am guilty of nothing more than existing and walking upon this earth, which I have every right to do."

Edmond joined Honor on the sofa, reaching across the red cushion to squeeze her hand. "Good for you. I might have known you would take a pragmatic view of the incident."

Trying to ignore the warmth that spread through her at

the touch of his strong fingers, she asked, "Where do you suppose Wade is hiding?"

"I wish I knew," he said, the words spoken through clenched teeth.

"So what do we do now?" Mr. Coverdale asked, his voice as calm as usual, though signs of anger showed in the stiffness of his posture and the taut pursing of his lips. "We cannot just sit here and wait until the scoundrel decides what new act of wickedness he wishes to visit upon us?"

"And we shall not do so," Edmond replied. Like Mr. Coverdale, he was not as relaxed as he appeared, for a muscle twitched in his firm jaw, and his eyes bore a hard, determined look. "I sent a letter to Bow Street, requesting a runner, but it could take as long as a week before anyone arrives."

"A good idea, nonetheless. But have you a plan for what we should do in the meantime?"

"In the meantime, I have instructed Traverchick to warn the staff to stay close to the house, and to do nothing foolish. And as many of the men as can use a firearm have been supplied with one. At the same time, it is my intention to—"

"In the meantime," Honor said, as though her uncle's question had been asked of her, "I think you and I should leave Raleigh Park."

Edmond's response was instantaneous. "Never!"

Denying herself the comfort of questioning his fervor, she asked rather hurriedly, "May I avail myself of that promised trip to town in your berlin?" When he made no reply, but stared at her as if he would like to shake her, she continued, "If you will ask someone to have the coach made ready, perhaps Uncle Wesley and I might leave this afternoon."

*   *   *

No amount of argument would sway Honor from her decision to leave, and though Edmond had said everything he could to persuade her that she would be safer at Raleigh Park—a belief shared by her uncle—she had not relented. Now she was in her bedchamber, preparing for the trip, which would commence directly a light nuncheon was served.

Because it was to be her last day there, and perhaps the last time she would ever be in Edmond Lawrence's company, Honor chose to don the new dress Celia had finished only the evening before. The material was a soft merino wool whose checked pattern of red and blue complimented Honor's almost black hair and dark blue eyes, and she was woman enough to admit she liked what she saw in her looking glass. That the frock's high waist and modest vee neckline fit her slender figure to perfection only added to her pleasure in the simple, yet elegant creation.

She had also laid out the lovely blue bonnet and its matching muff. She meant to wear them on her trip back to London, as much to look her best when she bade Edmond farewell as to show him that she had accepted his actions at the merchants not as machinations meant to rob her of her independence but as acts of kindness.

She was just pinning her mother's enamel watch to the bodice of the new dress when a knock sounded at the door. Having rung for the maid, she called out, "Come in, Celia, and see what a fine bird your fine feathers have made of me."

To her surprise, when the door was opened, one of the housemaids stepped just inside the room and bobbed a curtsy. "Begging your pardon, ma'am, but Celia bain't come back yet."

Knowing a moment of alarm, she said, "Come back? From where? I thought Mr. Lawrence gave explicit instructions that everyone was to stay close to the house."

"He did, ma'am. And bain't none of us in no hurry to venture out, not with a madman about the place."

Ignoring the dramatics, Honor said, "Then where is Celia?"

"She went down to the greenhouse, ma'am, to see if she could be of some use to Lady Raleigh. On account of her being the only one of us as has ever tended a flower garden, and her having a green thumb, as the saying goes, Cook said she could go ask her ladyship if she could help her and Eames."

Honor breathed a sigh of relief, glad the child was in no danger, for she was quite fond of the little carrot-top. "That was very kind of Celia."

"Yes'um. Be there aught I can do for you in Celia's place?"

"No, thank you." Not wanting it known throughout the house that she was leaving, not before the actual fact, Honor decided to do her own packing rather than ask the girl for help. "I merely wanted Celia to see her handiwork."

"And you look a picture, you do. If you'll forgive me saying so."

"Thank you." Smiling, Honor lifted her skirt slightly and made the young housemaid a curtsy, an action that caused the girl to giggle. "When Celia returns, please tell her to come up to my chamber."

"Yes, ma'am."

As soon as the maid left the room, closing the door behind her, Honor fetched her valise and quickly packed those items she had brought with her. Once that task was completed, she loosened the strings of her reticule and dumped the contents onto the bed, tossing the empty purse into the valise. Brushing aside a handkerchief, a card of pins, a small jar of almond balm she rubbed upon her lips to aid against chapping, and one or two other items, she soon found what she was looking for, the money she had meant to use for her stagecoach ticket to London.

Disregarding the six-pence, she picked up only the golden guinea and the five-pound note she had borrowed from Edmond the day she discovered him unconscious and alone in the overturned post chaise. Honor had no reason to worry about money now, for she would be traveling in the snug berlin with her uncle beside her, so before she left Raleigh Park, she meant to return the five-pound note. With that in mind, she folded the note and slipped it just inside the vee of her dress.

After placing the remaining items inside the pocket of the muff lining, all save the golden guinea, she laid the coin on the dressing table along with a note to Celia, just in case the maid did not return in time for Honor to give her the coin personally. Someone would be obliged to read the note to her, so Honor merely thanked her for her many kindnesses, saying nothing she would not wish everyone in the house to know.

With nothing else to detain her abovestairs, she left the bedchamber and walked across the carpeted landing to the broad, curving staircase. She had just placed her hand upon the polished mahogany banister when she saw Edmond come out of the drawing room and cross the vestibule, his destination the front entrance.

Pausing, she gave herself a moment to enjoy the assurance with which he carried himself, the grace of movement, the breadth of his back beneath the well-cut mulberry coat, and the supple bunching and relaxing of the muscles in his long legs as he strode purposefully toward the door.

He had already released the latch and opened the door a fraction of an inch, when he stopped. Almost as if he felt her watching him, Edmond turned slowly and looked up the wide staircase, directly at her.

His gaze was long and intense, as if measuring every inch of her from the crown of her head to the tip of her toes, and while he regarded her, Honor was robbed of the ability to breathe. Edmond continued to stare, the seconds stretching like hours, yet he seemed unabashed at any impropriety or rudeness on his part, aware of nothing save looking his fill.

As for Honor, she remained quite still, as though held in place by Edmond's mesmerizing scrutiny, her hand upon the banister, totally unable to take her eyes from his face.

When he closed the door and moved to the bottom of the staircase, she thought for a moment he meant to come up to her. He did not do so, however. Instead, he stopped just at the bottom step, and with a leisurely movement placed one booted foot on the stair. While one strong hand rested upon his bent knee, the other hand gripped the newel post, his long, tapered fingers idly caressing the smooth wood.

Though she called herself a fool for giving in to such fancy, it seemed to Honor that she felt the warmth of Edmond's hand travel up the smooth mahogany and touch her palm, the movement of his fingers sending shivers of delight up her arm and through her body.

He said not one word. And as their gazes locked, Honor thought she beheld in his brown eyes a look of undisguised longing. More fancy? Or was it simply the wish of her own heart imbuing him with the semblance of that emotion uppermost in her thoughts?

Silently, he watched her, and as if answering an unspoken summons—some primal invitation she was unable to refuse—Honor took the first step toward him. Drawn ever nearer, she descended the stairs until she was mere inches from him, their fingers almost touching on the banister.

"Did I ever tell you," he said, as though they had been in conversation all along, "of the first time I saw you?"

The simple question caused a wild fluttering within her rib cage. Powerless to speak, Honor merely shook her head.

"You stood at the foot of my bed," he said, "and at the time I was not certain if you were real or merely a figment of my fevered dreams." He paused, and when he spoke again, his voice was little more than a whisper. "Your hair was down."

The whispered phrase had an intimate sound, far more intimate than the fact of her having been in his room, her hair unbound.

"I have never seen such hair," he said, the words so soft, so hypnotic Honor was obliged to tighten her grip upon the handrail. "The brown was almost black, a mysterious color, and the strands were straight, yet supple as the blade of a fine sword."

His gaze slipped over her shoulders, as if still seeing the tresses as he remembered them. "It spilled down your back, flowing like layer upon layer of lustrous silk."

Like silk? The image left Honor's knees decidedly weak.

"Yes," he said, almost as if he had heard her thoughts.

He smiled at her, and it was a private smile, one she

had never seen before, almost as if it had been held in reserve for this moment, for her alone. "A good thing for you that I was too drugged to obey my baser impulses, for I was tempted to reach out and catch that dark silk, to feel its texture between my fingers, and to rub the smoothness of it against my lips."

His words set her heart to beating so wildly she thought it might burst right out of her chest, and it was all Honor could do not to reach up and pull the pins from the topknot, to let the hair fall where it would, on the chance that he might still wish to test it against his mouth.

Something in her eyes must have conveyed itself to him, for his own eyes widened, the brown of the pupils lit with emotion held in check. Then, with a movement that was purposeful, yet at the same time unhurried, he withdrew his foot from the bottom step, straightening to his full height. As he did so, Honor obeyed some inner feminine command, descending to the last stair and bringing their faces to the same level.

Giving her ample opportunity to back away if that was her wish, he moved slowly, lifting his large, strong hand from where it rested on the banister and placing it gently upon her forearm. Honor did not move, but waited breathlessly while he trailed his hand up her arm to her shoulder, letting it linger there a moment before slipping it around to the nape of her neck.

The touch of his fingers on her skin caused a languidness to invade Honor's limbs, making her long to lean against him, to feel his strength support her weight.

He seemed to know just what she wanted, and guiding his other hand around to the back of her waist, he slowly encouraged her to come to him.

"Edmond," she whispered, "I have wanted—"

"Brr," Simon Avery said as a blast of cold air from the

open doorway prompted Honor and Edmond to put some distance between them, "I believe the wind is picking up a bit."

"I think you are right, sir," replied a feminine voice, "for I feel frozen to the bone."

Only just noticing Edmond, the gentleman said, "Well met, old man. Glad we caught you, for Miss Moseby and I have a plan, one we think may serve. It was while we were riding about the estate that we came up with . . ."

He paused mid-sentence, only just realizing what he had interrupted. "I say. Forgive the intrusion, old man. Had no wish to—"

"Shut up, Avery."

Not in the least put out of countenance by such an impolite command, Mr. Avery looked up into the face of his friend and smiled. "Glad to. Nothing easier, I assure you. If you would like it, we could go out and come back in again."

Edmond had turned so that Honor was directly behind him, shielding her from view, giving her a moment to compose herself, but now she stepped onto the floor where she could see and be seen. "Dinah, where have you been? Have you spoken to Lady Raleigh?"

Dinah's lovely face was still pink from exposure to the cold air, but upon her lips was a smile as warm as a summer breeze. "Naturally I spoke to my mother. She and Mr. Avery and I had breakfast together. Or, I should say, we did *not* have breakfast together, for I could not swallow a bite, not after everything that had happened last evening, with that awful letter. And when I said I was not hungry, Mr. Avery declared himself without appetite as well."

Her story completed, the young lady granted the gentleman a smile guaranteed to make him wish to cry off food for a lifetime.

"Miss Moseby being a little upset, Lady Raleigh said I might have the pleasure of taking her for a sleigh ride, just across the estate, you understand, while there was still enough snow to make it possible. Of course, one of the grooms accompanied us. It was such a lovely drive, we would have taken longer, had the temperature not begun to drop." He smiled, "Not being made of sterner stuff, I was lured home by the promise of a mug of hot chocolate."

The pink of Dinah's cheeks suddenly became more intense, and she said, "Oh, Honor, I hope you do not think me insensitive for having gone for a pleasure ride when you were in such distress. But you were asleep, and we—"

"Dinah! Please be quiet."

The young lady was no more astounded by the request than was Mr. Avery. "No, really, ma'am. If anyone is to blame, it is I. Miss Moseby declined the invitation at first, but I—"

"Stubble it," Edmond suggested to his friend, "and let Honor speak."

She stepped over to Dinah and took both her gloved hands. "Something distressing had occurred."

"You mean the letter?"

Honor shook her head. "Something else."

Dinah's green eyes suddenly wide with apprehension, she said, "Where is my mother?"

"Your mother is fine," Edmond said, the authority in his voice lending credence to the statement. "She has merely sustained a shock."

Noting the girl's sudden pallor, Honor hurried to assure her that it was nothing physical, telling her in as few words as possible what had happened. "It was an unconscionable act of vandalism, and as you can imagine, Lady Raleigh was quite upset to discover the condition of the plants and flowers. She and Eames are at the greenhouses now, sorting through the debris, seeing what can be saved."

Dinah seemed momentarily unable to speak; however, Mr. Avery was quick to intercede on her behalf, asking his question of Edmond. "And no one was injured in this vandalism?"

"Not physically, at any rate. Unfortunately, Rowina is much distressed, as you can imagine."

The girl's lips trembled, but she tried bravely to keep control of her emotions. Placing her hand on Mr. Avery's arm, she said, "Thank you for the drive, but you must excuse me now. I wish to go to my mother."

"Not alone!" Edmond said.

"She will not," Mr. Avery replied quietly, reading in his friend's eyes the seriousness of the situation.

"Have a care," Edmond cautioned, "for we have no way of knowing where this man is or what he may be planning next. As you can imagine, he—"

His words were interrupted by the opening of the front door. "Mother!" Dinah said, throwing herself into her parent's arms. "Are you all right?"

Lady Rowina returned her daughter's embrace, then put her away gently. "I am filthy child. I have come back only to see if Cousin Edmond would grant me leave to have one or two of the servants come down to help in the greenhouses. The job is more than Eames and I can possibly do alone."

"Of course," Edmond replied, "you have only to choose whom you wish."

"Alone?" Honor said. "You meant to say, yourself, Eames, and Celia, did you not?"

Lady Raleigh stared at her. "Celia? Whatever do you mean? I have not seen Celia since this morning, just before breakfast."

Chapter 14

At the lady's words, Honor knew a moment of sick emptiness inside her stomach. "But Celia went down to the greenhouse to see if you wanted her assistance. One of the housemaids told me not ten minutes ago that Cook had given Celia permission to do so."

Rowina pressed her soiled fingers to her lips. "Oh, no," she said, her voice hushed. "I have seen no one at the greenhouse since you and the gentlemen left more than an hour ago."

At just that moment Mr. Coverdale emerged from the library, and seeing everyone gathered in the vestibule, he hastened forward. "What is amiss?" he asked. "Has there been another message from Wade?"

Leaving the others to answer her uncle's questions, Honor turned and hurried down the corridor toward the kitchen.

"Sir," Lady Raleigh answered, "one of the maids may be missing."

He would have followed his niece had Edmond not caught his arm. "Let me, sir. I will return in a minute."

Following Honor through the servants' hall to the kitchen, he arrived just in time to hear the cook give vent to a loud screech that sent the scullary maid in hot pursuit of hartshorn and feathers.

"Lawks! My poor little Celia!" Dissolving into tears, the woman muttered from behind her plump fingers, "What shall I tell my sister? Fair dotes on the girl, she does."

Edmond was about to admonish the woman to get a hold on her emotions, but he abandoned the idea when he saw Honor ignore the cook and quietly pull one of the housemaids over to the far corner of the room. He followed them, letting Honor do the questioning.

"Are you certain?" she said, "that Celia left to go to the greenhouse?"

Frightened to be singled out by both the mistress and the master of the house, the girl bobbed a curtsy and nodded her head again and again, causing the ruffles of her mobcap to flap like a puppet on a string. "I saw her leave with my own eyes, ma'am. Took time to put on her pattens, she did, so she could go the short way across the kitchen garden without getting her boots muddy."

"Then you did not actually see her reach the gravel path?"

"No, ma'am. But the greenhouse be her destination, right enough. She just took the shortcut, is all."

That sick feeling inside Honor's stomach grew, causing her to swallow once or twice before she could speak. "He has her," she said so softly Edmond could only just hear her. "Wade must have been watching the greenhouses."

Edmond cursed, paying little heed to the number of females he scandalized with his profanity. "We cannot be certain of that. I will have all the available men search the area. We may well discover that the girl has simply taken a little time for herself. Perhaps she has a young man in the neighborhood."

Honor looked hopefully toward the housemaid. "Has she a young man?"

The maid shook her head. "No, ma'am. Not Celia. She wouldn't have aught to do with any of the lads around here."

The cook's dramatics suddenly gave over, replaced by familial indignation. Her ample frame suddenly rigid with anger, she informed any who cared to listen that she would not stand for any scandalizing of her name. "A good Christian girl, be our Celia. And she bain't the kind as would go off without permission."

"Of course she is not," Honor agreed. "Mr. Lawrence meant no slur against your family. He does not know Celia as we do."

Mollified, the cook suddenly burst into sincere tears, the sound distracting them so they were not immediately aware of Eames opening the back door. Obviously surprised to see so many people congregated, the wizened little man stopped on the threshold.

Edmond was the first to find his voice. "What is it?"

Doffing his cap, the gardener motioned toward Edmond, implying that he would like to see him outside. Heeding the summons, Edmond followed the man, but when he would have shut the door, Honor was there, forcing her way out as well.

"What has happened?" she asked.

The little man looked to Edmond for guidance, and at his nod produced something from behind his back. It was a starched mobcap. From the way the man held it, his grimy fingers keeping the edges shut tight, it was obvious that something lay inside.

Some premonition, some dread so vile it would not be ignored, prompted Honor to reach for the once pristine cap, and thought Edmond issued a gruff order for her to stop, the gardener had already surrendered his burden before he could withdraw his hand. Instantly, Edmond reached out and caught Honor's wrist, his strong fingers digging into her flesh so fiercely that she was obliged to let him take the cap.

"Do no look!" he ordered.

Turning his back so that she could not see what he was doing, Edmond examined the contents of the mobcap. All Honor heard was his swiftly indrawn breath.

"What is it? Please, Edmond, I must know."

He turned back to her, his face registering relief, and held the cap open so she could see its contents. Inside lay a woman's braid, the foot or more of hair sawn through roughly, as though the excision had been performed by a dull knife. The carroty red of the hair shone in the sunlight like a piece of polished copper.

Honor did not ever want to know what Edmond had feared lay in the cap, especially since he was evidently relieved by what he found, but for her the braid was obscene enough to send a shiver of revulsion through her. "The animal! Poor Celia must be frightened out of her wits."

Edmond shoved the cap and its contents inside his coat, where they were out of sight. "Do not worry. We will find the girl."

Her knees suddenly shaking so badly she feared she might fall, Honor reached behind her to grip the thick iron door handle. Leaning her weight against the rough stone of the surrounding frame, she muttered, "I should have left as soon as I received the letter. Only see what the delay has wrought."

No amount of argument on Honor's part would convince Edmond that she should accompany him and Mr.

Avery and the four male servants who made up the search party, even though she followed him from the drawing room to the vestibule, still pleading her case. Initially, he had refused to take her along because he wanted her to remain at home where she would be safe, out of harm's way, but now that conviction was strengthened by her latest suggestion, a plan which he did not scruple to stigmatize as "A damned idiotic notion."

"Under no circumstances will I allow you to trade places with Celia, so you may put that notion right out of your head."

Unmindful of their audience, she caught his sleeve, forcing him to stop his progress to the door. "But what if Wade will not release her otherwise?"

"He will release her."

Edmond's face was unreadable, as if he had donned a sort of mental armor, and Honor decided that one might be forgiven for thinking him unmoved, were it not for the occasional clenching of a muscle in his right jaw.

She sighed, frustrated by her inability to make him understand the complexity of the man he must face. "You do not know Jerome Wade. He is quite cunning. And tenacious as a wild animal stalking his prey. He believes himself indomitable. Unstoppable."

"Then I must disabuse him of that notion."

"But—"

He placed his finger across her lips, gently putting an end to her protests. "I intend to catch Mr. Jerome Wade, Esquire, and bring the maid home. And I shall do so with greater ease if I am not called upon to restrain you from performing some quite unnecessary act of heroism."

To no one's surprise, least of all Honor's, both her uncle and Mr. Avery concurred with Edmond's mandate that she should remain behind. And to add insult to injury, Dinah gave it as her opinion that gentlemen always knew best.

Honor was on the verge of informing one and all what she thought of such high-handed interference, when Edmond said, "Let us speak no more of it. You will please me by remaining here." And though the phrasing was polite enough, his authoritative tone left none of those gathered in the small area in any doubt about his having once been a military officer.

"Remember," he said, as though giving orders to young subalterns, "the doors are to be locked, and no one is to leave the house for any reason. I do not wish any of you to take unnecessary risks."

He looked particularly at Honor when he said this, but she stared right back at him, her head held high, unintimidated by his manner. When he put his hand beneath her elbow and led her a little way down the corridor to bid her a private farewell, she asked rather waspishly, "Does that warning about unnecessary risks apply to yourself as well?"

Apparently he was not put off in the least by her sharp tone, for a slow smile pulled at his lips, and all vestiges of warrior grimness vanished from his face. "Am I to understand," he asked softly, "that you are concerned for my welfare?"

Not unmoved by that smile, or the soft, insinuating words, she relented somewhat. "I should be unforgivably heartless if I were not concerned—for the welfare of the entire party."

He chuckled. "A commendable sentiment, my dear."

When an answering smile threatened her own lips, she lowered her head so that he could not see her face. He was not misled, and with his free hand, he took her chin and lifted it so that he could look into her eyes, gazing into the blue depths as if searching for something. If he found what he sought, she could not say, but a gleam of humor lit the depths of his brown eyes as they focused on hers.

Leaning close to her ear so that only she could hear his words, he said, "When I return, remind me to tell you about that lake in Portugal."

According to the little enamel watch, which she checked at increasingly shorter intervals, the search party had not been gone above an hour. Unfortunately for Honor's nerves, the arrow-tipped minute hand appeared to be moving at a snail's pace, while the heart inside her breast seemed to be racing faster and faster until she thought it would explode.

Hoping a bit of exercise might alleviate the stress upon her nerves, she rose from the pianoforte, where she had been idly strumming chords, and walked across to look out the French windows. To her disappointment, all she saw when she pushed aside the thick red drapery was the snow-covered lawn and the leafless branches of the elms that swayed in the freshening wind.

"I am persuaded that Celia will be just fine," Dinah said, looking up from a copy of *Waverley*.

"I quite agree," Lady Raleigh said, sparing a moment from the quiet coze in which she and Uncle Wesley were engaged. "And though your concern for the maid does you credit, Honor, my dear, it will benefit Celia none at all for you to make yourself sick with worry."

Muttering some response, Honor turned from her contemplation of the front lawn and walked the length of the drawing room, then continued through the mahogany pocket doors that divided the more formal room from the wainscoted library. Caring little if she appeared rude, she closed the doors, thinking she could endure the wait better if she were not also required to endure well-meant platitudes.

Thankful to be alone, where she need not hide her anxiety, Honor strolled around the quiet room, lifting a book now and then, but not bothering to read the title before setting each volume back on the shelf. After a time she arrived at the French doors were she idly twirled a globe of the Earth that stood on the marble pedestal, all the while staring, unseeing, into the hedge-enclosed rear garden.

Soon tiring of the globe, Honor turned and strode over to the well-used oak writing desk where she picked up Edmond's pen. Holding the quill with both hands, she indulged herself in the quite fanciful notion that she could still feel the warmth of his fingers upon the shaft.

Dinah and Rowina had been slightly off the mark in their assumption that her concern was for Celia alone. She was anxious for the maid, there was no denying that fact, but it was her fear for Edmond that made her heart pound painfully.

Edmond was powerfully built and trained in the art of war, and he was secure in his belief that should he and Jerome Wade meet, he would best the barrister. Unfortunately, Honor was not so confident, for although Edmond had the advantage in both strength and knowledge, he was also an honorable man, accustomed to dealing with gentlemen, and therein lay his disadvantage. He had no idea the kind of devious, depraved person he would be facing.

Lost in her concern for Edmond's safety, Honor was unaware of the stealthy movement just outside the French windows. Her first indication that she was not alone was a sudden splintering noise behind her, followed by a burst of icy air. Yet even before she whirled around, some inner voice told her what to expect. It was as if her thoughts of the barrister had conjured him up, for Jerome Wade stood only a few feet away, his arm inside the door, releasing the lock. An instant later, pieces of broken glass crunched beneath his boots as he entered the library.

His blond hair was mussed by the wind, lending him a quite deceptive air of boyish innocence, and his usually cold gray eyes were alight with victory.

"So," he said, "I have found you at last."

Honor's racing heart slammed against her ribs, then seemed to stop altogether. She took a step back, her one wish to escape to the drawing room where the others sat blissfully unaware that evil incarnate had just invaded the house.

So much for my career as a heroine!

Looking at the man, she wondered how she could have considered, even for a moment, placing herself in his hands. True, she had wanted to save Celia, but now she wanted nothing so much as to flee from this fiend's presence.

Wade must have sensed her thoughts, for he raised his arm, revealing the implement he had used to smash the glass in the French door. At the sight of it, Honor gasped, for in his right hand he held a pistol, and it was aimed directly at her.

When he spoke again, Honor was amazed at how calm he sounded, how reasonable, as though he argued a case in court, a case he felt certain he would win. "I told you once before, *cara mia,* when you admired my walking stick, that I carried the weapon only for those who would cross me. So it is with the pistol."

He smiled, his manner congenial, as if relating an amusing story for the entertainment of like-minded friends. "There are those who hold the opinion that the handgun is not nearly so refined as the sword, and in the case of gentlemanly disputes, I concur. But one must admit that firearms are much more effective when one's quarry is at a distance."

The smile disappeared, replaced by a look so cold, so dispassionate, that it sent waves of fear crashing through Honor. Slowly, purposefully, he moved his arm so the pistol was pointed in the direction of the drawing room. "If you choose to cross me," he said, "I will shoot the first person who walks through those doors."

Chapter 15

Honor had never known such fear. She seemed to be drowning in it, unable to catch her breath. "What do you want?" she asked, the halting words quivering so badly she barely recognized her own voice.

"Want?" He shrugged his elegantly clad shoulders, the many capes of his wool surtout rising as he did so. "I want what I have always wanted, *cara*. You. And now, I shall have you."

His careless assumption that she was his for the taking—like a piece of merchandise in a shop—sent a surge of anger through her, anger that buoyed her flagging spirits. "But I do not want *you*. Would you have a woman who finds you repugnant in every way?"

He smiled, but the expression on his face was without joy. "Have a care what you say, *cara,* for you have led me an exhaustive chase, and my forbearance is near its end. You will soon discover that when I am put out of patience, I am not always kind. At such times I might be tempted to make you pay for any thoughtless remarks."

The quietly stated threat chilled Honor to the bone, effectively dissolving her anger, and leaving her with the suspicion that fear was a bottomless pit. She hoped never to reach the lowest point of that pit, but she did not want to let him know how much the thought disturbed her, so she asked, "Where is Celia?"

He appeared surprised by the question. "I do not know anyone by that name. You must be—"

"The maid. You sent her braid, did you not?"

"Ah, yes. The red-haired child. A spunky little thing. Normally, I find such resistance invigorating, but in this case it was ill-timed. I was forced to restrain her. For her own good, you understand. She seemed bent upon returning to you."

As if the maid were of no value, something to be used then discarded, he said, "I left her at an old deserted cottage near an apple orchard."

Anger flared once again inside Honor. "If you have hurt her, I promise you will pay."

The thin veneer of his civility was suddenly whisked away, and Honor saw the snarling beast beneath. "How dare you threaten me!"

Moving more quickly than she would have thought possible in one whose manner had always appeared languid in the extreme, Jerome Wade reached out and grabbed her by the neck, his thumb pressing into her throat so cruelly she was unable to draw breath.

When she thought she must surely faint from lack of air, he made one final push against her windpipe; then smiling with pleasure, he released her.

Honor slumped against the desk, gasping painfully.

"One must always know how far is too far," he said, as though instructing her in some art. "Unlike the impatient cat who kills his mouse, thus leaving himself without a toy, I have learned when to let my playthings have a moment to recuperate."

Capturing her neck once again, he began moving his thumb in small circles, stroking the tender skin he had so ruthlessly bruised. "Did it hurt?" he asked. "Your pardon, *cara mia*."

Honor thought she might be sick, so revolted was she by his touch. Suddenly filled with anger that he should take such liberties against her will, she slapped at his wrist. "Take your hands off me!"

To her surprise, he released her, laughing as he did so. "So, the little mouse roars. Such fun we shall have, once we are back in London. You and I will explore the very boundaries of ecstasy; sensations never so—"

Whatever he had meant to say, it was interrupted by the sound of excited voices coming from the front of the house.

"Honor!" Dinah called, rapping at the pocket doors. "Hurry, do. The gentlemen have returned, and they have got Celia with them."

For just a moment Honor considered crying out, but immediately Jerome Wade caught her by the arm and yanked her to her feet, shoving the barrel of the handgun into her ribs. Without saying a word, he made his way to the French doors, forcing her to come along with him.

When they were outside on the flagstone path that serpentined across the small garden, he thrust Honor in front of him, urging her to move quickly by jabbing her between the shoulder blades with the pistol.

"Keep moving," he ordered.

"Where are we going?"

"For now, just beyond the garden. You will find my horse tied to an elm tree on the other side of the hedge. Of course, we shall be obliged to ride double until we reach The Two Swans at Abbingdon. But have no fear, for the gelding is well built and can carry our weight, and I shall hold you snugly against me, lest you fear for your safety. The moment we arrive at the inn, I shall hire a post chaise to convey us to London."

Trying not to think of what he might do once they were within the confines of a closed carriage, Honor hurried toward the bottom of the garden. Because of the sudden drop in temperature, the water that had flowed across the flagstones due to the earlier melting snow was now turning to ice. Slipping once or twice, she fought to maintain her balance, afraid that if she fell, Wade might decide she had *crossed* him, and retaliate with a bullet to her back.

Without a wrap of any kind to protect her from the bitter cold, she shivered, and as she panted from both fear and exertion, she could see her breath hang upon the air.

"Please," she said as they reached the end of the serpentine path and pushed their way through a break in the hedge, "let me go. If I am exposed to this weather for long, I shall very likely contract pneumonia."

He did not even bother to answer.

"Over there," he said, pointing toward a large elm and an ill-used roan gelding tied to one of the low branches. The animal had obviously been ridden hard and left with a wet coat, and after standing in the wind for some time, its nostrils were beginning to crust over with ice crystals. Watching it paw the ground nervously, Honor knew a moment of fellow-feeling with the creature, which, like her, was in the power of a man who possessed not a shred of human compassion.

"Step lively," Wade said.

Approaching the horse, Honor noted a pair of saddle-bags, and protruding from one of the pouches was the walking stick with the ivory wolf's head. She had thought she could not be any more frightened, yet spying the stick, and remembering the concealed weapon, lent an added dimension to her fear.

"Here," Wade said, slipping the pistol inside his surtout, then cupping his hands to accommodate her foot, "I'll toss you into the saddle, then as soon as I am mounted, we can be on our way."

While frantically seeking a reason not to put her foot into his waiting hands, knowing once she left Raleigh Park there would be little hope of anyone finding her, something prompted her to look beyond the man's shoulder, back toward the garden. Afraid her imagination might be playing a cruel hoax upon her, she blinked. To her almost unbearable relief, what she saw was no mirage, but a man whose countenance resembled nothing so much as an enraged bull. No more than a dozen yards separated them, and as Edmond ran toward her, the gap narrowed quickly.

Hearing the muted thud of boots pounding upon the hard earth, Jerome Wade dropped his cupped hands and turned toward the sound, at the same time reaching inside his coat for the pistol. Slowed by the heavy wool of the surtout, the handgun had only just cleared Wade's pocket when Edmond charged at him, headfirst, dealing him a punishing blow that knocked him off his feet and sent the weapon flying, to be lost somewhere beneath the hedge.

In the melee that followed, Edmond had the physical advantage over Jerome Wade, though the barrister was surprisingly skillful with his fists, holding his own in the battle. While the men pounded at one another, grunting and cursing, the poor gelding nearly lost its wits. Already frightened, the animal tossed its large head and sidestepped nervously, trying to pull free, and though

Honor tried to get out of the beast's way, it chanced to hit her shoulder with its head, knocking her to her knees.

On all fours, she scurried out of the reach of the powerful hooves, and was still trying to get to her feet when she saw Edmond slip on an icy patch and fall to the ground, the sudden impact leaving him momentarily stunned. While he lay thus, attempting to clear his head, Jerome Wade ran over to the horse, grabbed a handful of mane to force the skittish gelding into submission, then yanked the walking stick from the saddlebag.

Though Wade's handsome face glistened with sweat, a look of pure malice, as cold and unforgiving as the frozen wastelands of the poles, shone in his eyes. With a smile he pressed the button beneath the wolf's ivory head and withdrew the concealed sword from the hollow stick.

"And now," he yelled triumphantly, brandishing the sword, then pointing it toward Edmond, "prepare to meet your Maker."

As Wade flung the empty stick aside, the gelding laid back its ears, snorting in terror. With a fierce jerk of its head it broke the reins and reared up on its hind legs, one of its hooves hitting the barrister in the back of the head.

For one awful moment Jerome Wade stared at Honor, a look of total surprise in his eyes.

"Help me," he whispered. Then, still clutching the sword, he pitched forward, landing facedown on the cold ground.

"But I tell you, I am unharmed," Honor said. "It is but a bruised shoulder. By tomorrow I shall not even notice it."

"I still want the doctor to look at it," her uncle said. "He is already here, so why not indulge me?"

At her sigh of resignation Mr. Coverdale walked over to her bedchamber door and ushered in the white-haired physician who resided in Abbingdon. "What of the man?" he asked quietly.

"Dead," the doctor answered. "Nothing anyone can do for a fellow who gets himself kicked in the head. Not but what I would have been tempted to kick him myself, the way he treated that poor horse."

Wesley Coverdale nodded, keeping his thoughts to himself, for a verdict of accidental death suited him just fine. There was nothing to be gained by telling the entire, sordid story, and as far as he was concerned, justice had been served. "So you will make the arrangements to have the deceased conveyed to his home in London?"

"Of course. Already sent him back to Abbingdon to be seen to properly. Mr. Lawrence very kindly supplied one of the estate wagons and a couple of grooms to see to the job. Took the horse back, too," he added.

Grateful to know that Wade was off the property, and that they need concern themselves with him no longer, he led the doctor to the blue chair where Honor sat before a roaring fire. "Come," he said, "let me make you known to my niece."

To Honor's relief, the doctor's examination took less than two minutes. "Have your maid rub camphor liniment on any areas that are stiff or bruised," he said. "And next time, mind your step. A fall on the ice can be quite serious."

"I will be more careful," she replied meekly, glad that someone had invented a plausible reason for her injuries.

Just before he closed the door, the elderly gentleman eyed the pretty lace-trimmed wrapper she wore, the wrapper Celia had finished just minutes earlier and insisted she don in place of the soiled dress. "If you want my advice," he said, "put on something warm. And in future, do not go outside without a proper coat."

Once the doctor was gone, she asked her uncle, "Have we any camphor liniment at home? I do not recall ever seeing any."

Ignoring the question of the liniment, he said rather hesitantly, "Regarding our return to London, I think we should hold up on that for a while."

"How long a while?"

He did not answer her right away, but studied his hands, giving special attention to the tips of his fingers, appearing, for want of a better word, embarrassed. "Edmond has offered me a position here."

Honor could not believe her ears. "Are you roasting me, Uncle?"

"No, child. Edmond has little faith in his man of business, so he asked me if I would consider staying here and aiding him in that capacity."

"Here? In this house?"

"For a time, at least. He has offered to have a small house built for me, on a pretty knoll quite near the apple orchard." He paused for a moment, his gaze still not meeting hers. "The house would be within easy walking distance of the greenhouses."

"The greenhouses? But why . . ."

She stopped, suddenly remembering Rowina Raleigh's musings about why a wonderful man like Wesley Coverdale had never married. As well, she recalled those little quiet talks the two of them seemed always to be enjoying. "Uncle Wesley. Are you and Lady Raleigh . . . what I mean to say is, does she . . ."

"It is early days yet, my dear. For one thing, Rowina's year of mourning for Sir Frederick is not yet over. However, when that period is concluded, we may have an interesting announcement. In the meantime, it is enough that Edmond has made his two quite generous offers."

"And what of me? Where am I supposed to go?" Though she was embarrassed to ask such a selfish question, Honor needed to know the answer.

Her uncle's face was impassive. "Perhaps that is a matter you should discuss with someone else."

Having said this, he rose from the chair and went over to the dressing room door and rapped softly upon it. Not waiting for a reply, he strode over to the far door and left the room.

Within a matter of seconds Edmond stood in the dressing room doorway. Honor had not seen him since the two of them had been helped back to the house by the men of the search party. In that time he had cleaned up and changed his clothes, but the evidence of his fight with Jerome Wade still showed upon his face. A court plaster covered a cut on his right jaw, and his left eye was beginning to color.

"May I come in?" he asked.

Remembering how he had fought for her, and suffered injury at the barrister's hands, how could she say him nay? Not that she wished to, of course. What she wanted to say was, *Come take me in your arms. Hold me close and never let me go.* But she could not say that; not when he did not love her. Not when she loved him to distraction.

She watched him stroll over to the fireplace, where he leaned his shoulder against the mantel, staring into the flames. After a time, when he continued to look everywhere but at her she cleared her throat meaningfully to gain his attention.

"Thank you," she said, "for saving me."

Edmond muttered something beneath his breath, then

turned and regarded her, though she almost wished he had not, for the agony in his eyes was more than she could bear.

"I feared I might lose you," he said. "When I arrived home and found the door broken and you gone, I nearly went out of my mind. I have never been so frightened in my life. Not even in the war." He stopped, his breathing ragged. "Then I saw that . . . that *animal,* with his hands on you, and I . . ."

"Oh, Edmond. I—"

"Do not leave," he whispered. "Stay. Marry me."

Honor felt tears sting her eyes. He was asking her again, giving her another opportunity to spend her life with him.

But, of course, she could not.

When she would have spoken, he stopped her. "Do not answer yet. Please. I know I made a botch of the proposal yesterday. I said all the wrong things and left out the things that were most important."

"You did?"

He gave her a wry smile. "You know that I did. For one thing, I never told you how much I love you."

Honor could not credit what she had just heard. "But you . . . you do not love me."

He raised a questioning brow. "I do not? And just where did you come up with that idiotic notion?"

Hope rose inside her at this unloverlike remark. "Is it? Idiotic, I mean."

She watched him, her heart beating wildly at the thought that he meant what he said, that he was not just telling her whatever was necessary to get her to agree to marry him.

"Honor Danforth, I have never loved anyone as I love you."

Seeing the way he looked at her, his brown eyes curiously tender, she knew he spoke the truth, and when he held out his hand, she rose and went to him, putting her hand in his. Gently, he tugged her closer, until he was able to place her palm flat against his heart.

"Feel that," he said. "It nearly stopped beating today."

"Shh," she said, shaking her head. She did not want to think about Jerome Wade. Not now, not ever again.

He seemed to understand her need, for he reached out and pulled her into his arms, holding her tightly. At his touch a delicious feeling of safety enveloped her. After a time, however, when his lips descended, covering hers and drawing from her the love and passion she had longed to give, safety was the last thing on her mind.

As their kiss deepened, her entire body quivered with life, while her soul seemed to meld with his.

Some minutes later, he pushed her away, and with a voice husky with emotion, he asked her once again to marry him.

"Yes," she said, her own voice none too steady.

"Right away?"

She thought she must surely be dreaming, for how else could she be so happy? "As soon as possible," she replied.

"A special license would be best, I think. That way we can be married wherever and whenever we choose. I can leave first thing tomorrow and be back in just a few days."

To Edmond's surprise she would not hear of his going without her.

"I am not letting you out of my sight," she said. "The last time you traveled alone, all manner of terrible things happened to you. Which reminds me of something."

To his astonishment, she reached her fingers inside the

pretty lace wrapper she wore and removed a five-pound note. "I meant to give this to you earlier. It belongs to you."

The money was still warm from its contact with her soft flesh, and Edmond was forced to remind himself that they were not yet married. Taking a steadying breath, he said, "Thank you. You are a most honorable lady."

"Not really," she said, a twinkle in her eyes. "I am actually quite shameless."

"Is that so?" he asked, captivated by the thought.

"Yes, for I want another kiss, and I do not mind asking for it."

As she attempted to wind her arms around his waist, he caught her by the shoulders, holding her so that she could not get any closer. "Have a care, my love, for I am but a mere mortal." Giving her a chaste kiss on the forehead, he said, "There, that will have to do you until we are married."

"I protest," she said. "If it is to be my last kiss for what could be days, surely you can do better than that."

She pouted adorably, pursing her soft lips in a way that very nearly drove him insane. When she looked up at him, pleading silently with those beautiful blue eyes, he was not able to resist. Taking her in his arms, he kissed her again.

When the kiss finally ended, Honor sighed contentedly.

"Better?" he asked softly.

She nodded. "That, my darling man, was most definitely better."